Murder, Lies & Innocence Lost

A Novel by

John W. Gemmer

CCB Publishing
British Columbia, Canada

Murder, Lies & Innocence Lost: A Novel

ISBN-13 978-1-77143-469-0
First Edition

Library and Archives Canada Cataloguing in Publication
Title: Murder, lies & innocence lost / a novel by John W. Gemmer.
Other titles: Murder, lies and innocence lost
Names: Gemmer, John W., 1948- author.
Description: First edition.
Identifiers: Canadiana (print) 20210114274 | Canadiana (ebook) 20210114339
| ISBN 9781771434690 (softcover) | ISBN 9781771434706 (PDF)
Classification: LCC PS3607.E55 M87 2021 | DDC 813/.6—dc23

Cover artwork: Amish buggy © wico | CanStockPhoto.com

Publisher: CCB Publishing
British Columbia, Canada
www.ccbpublishing.com

Dedication

This book is being dedicated to the memory of one of my best friends, Kevin A. Sheets, who helped to start my writing career. Kevin passed away on August 10, 2020 from a genetic lung disease and I continue to miss his friendship, humor, and intellect. Rest in peace, Kevin!

Acknowledgements

Special thanks to Hope Heritz, my significant other, Sandra Snyder, a retired Captain on the Detective Bureau of the Goshen (Indiana) Police Department, R.T. Snyder, a retired Major on the Detective Bureau of the Elkhart (Indiana) County Sheriff's Department, Jeff Rasley, my very talented editor, and Paul Rabinovitch, my helpful publisher, CCB Publishing, British Columbia, Canada. Without their help I would not have been able to write and publish this book to my satisfaction. Their help was invaluable to me in completing *Murder, Lies & Innocence Lost*.

Books by John W. Gemmer

The Last Assignment

Harsh Consequences

Terrorists in the Heartland

Evil Lives Among Us

The Secret Pact

Murder, Lies & Innocence Lost

Preface

My latest novel is a fictional story about a homicide that takes place in an Amish community. This book was not written to criticize any particular segment of our community, but rather to illuminate the unique differences and habits between what the Amish call the "English" or non-Amish and themselves. It also illustrates how the Amish interact in a diverse society. These aspects of Amish life are woven into a tale about the death of an Amish girl, which takes place in an Amish family's barn.

All people sin, whether they're Anabaptists, Catholics, Protestants, Muslims, Hindus, or Jews, and that includes me. And, we all behave badly during fits of rage, which might lead to committing criminal activity. Criminal activity resides in every community. Criminals might or might not be affiliated with a particular religious group. Our legal system has been promulgated to deal with criminal offenses.

In the case of the Old Order Amish, they live by God's laws first, before adhering to man's. Amish folks are less likely to report crimes to the authorities. One reason is their belief in the "two kingdom doctrine", which is the belief that Christians should remain apart from the world. So, the Amish try to handle issues internally.

This is another one of my books about murder. Or, does it end up not being murder after all? You'll find out, if you read this novel. Please enjoy the story. Once again, I've tried to introduce sufficient twists and turns into the plot to maintain your interest. I have purposely contrived to confuse and entertain the readers of my stories involving murder plots and criminal activities. Thank you for purchasing my book. And, if possible, please write a review and post it on the Amazon.com website.

Murder, Lies & Innocence Lost

Chapter 1

Clarence J. Moore awoke at sunrise on Saturday morning. He looked over at his pretty wife Jean, who was still asleep next to him in the king-sized bed. He admired her naked form for a moment. The alarm clock read 7:28 a.m. Sunlight was beginning to trickle through the bedroom windows. It reminded him that they needed to go shopping for window coverings. He could see the fog slowly rising off the crystal-clear lake through the large picture window in the open loft master suite. The previous evening, the couple celebrated their relocation to Ohio in their new home with an intimate candle light dinner. After a delicious beef tenderloin meal, prepared outside on a charcoal grill, they drank a few too many cocktails and the evening ended with passionate love-making. Jean drank more than she could handle.

Clarence had turned off the alarm clock prior to falling asleep, so Jean could sleep-in longer than usual. He knew she'd have a hangover and would need additional rest. He carefully got out of bed, put on a robe, and quietly went downstairs to make a cup of tea for himself.

The couple packed and moved from their Chicago, Illinois residence to Grant County in the northwestern corner of Ohio on August 13, 1988. They stayed in a bed and breakfast during their search for a home. After a week of house shopping, they toured a freshly listed 1,350 square foot newly constructed A-frame house that was on the market. The A-frame house was built on an acre lot, which also featured a small storage shed located near the back of the lot. Several maple trees, flowering plants, and bushes were added to the property by the seller to enhance the curb appeal. The moment the realtor showed them the listing they fell in love with the house and lot.

The home featured a large living room, kitchen and dining area, laundry area, and a guest bedroom on the main floor. They especially liked the lake view from the spacious second-floor master suite. They made a full-price offer the day they toured the Hancock Lake property and moved in a week later. The house was built on Hancock Lake, a 355-acre all-sports lake. Hancock is the largest lake in a chain of five lakes, sometimes called the Interstate Lakes because they flow through Ohio to Indiana.

Prior to moving to Grant County, they lived in Edgewater, one of the nicer neighborhoods in Chicago. Edgewater had been the Moore's residence for the past five years. Clarence and Jean lived in Edgewater to be close to his ailing mother, Bessie Moore. But when Bessie suddenly passed, the couple decided to make a move. Clarence knew Edgewater was a good place to live and raise a family, but he and Jean both wanted a change from their hectic lifestyle in Chicago.

Clarence married Jean Turner, when he was thirty-one years old. Jean was blue-eyed, high-spirited, raven-haired, and five-foot eight inches tall without heels. She was attractive with an athletic physique. As a mid-level retail executive, she ran three small department stores in the Chicago area. The couple intended to start a family someday. Jean was two years younger than Clarence. She was a rising star in her corporation. When a better employment opportunity became available for Jean, they decided the time was right to take a chance and move. Several months later, they packed their things and moved to a rural location in Grant County on the Ohio/Indiana/Michigan borders.

Northwestern Ohio seemed quaint, affordable, and perfect for raising a family. Jean's new position was to oversee six department stores in Indiana, Ohio, and Michigan. This would require more travel time for her, but the move was a great opportunity for Jean. Grant County was centrally located to the six stores she would manage as a newly appointed regional vice president. Grant County shares its borders with Gallian County to the east, the state of Indiana to the west, Ports County to the south, and the state of Michigan to the north.

The city of Wayne, Ohio has been the Grant County seat since an act of the Ohio Legislature in 1820. According to county records, the population of Grant County was approximately 29,477 in 1980. The population growth rate was 8.37 percent. The predominately flat terrain of Grant County encompasses vast expanses of farmland, dense forests, and glacier-formed small lakes. There are several small villages and hamlets in rural Grant

County, in addition to the city of Wayne.

In 1985, the racial makeup of the county was 96.6 percent white and 3.4 percent for all others. In terms of ancestry, the county is comprised of mostly Amish, German, Irish, and English descent. The significant businesses in Grant County were agricultural endeavors, accessory manufacturing for the automotive industry, restaurants, and small tourism shops mainly located in the town of Wayne, Ohio. There was a small accredited college of close to a thousand students on campus in the city of Wayne. Not surprisingly, it was called Wayne College.

Grant County is governed by three elected commissioners, a sheriff, coroner, auditor, treasurer, clerk of the court of common pleas prosecutor, engineer, and recorder. Grant is within Ohio's 1st Congressional District and has been a Republican stronghold for years.

A large Amish population has inhabited the area for well over a hundred years. Largely because of interest in the Amish, tourism is one of the major businesses in Grant County. The area is also well-known for its automotive accessory manufacturers. Those specialized industries have become the major employers in the county. There are several other all-sports, glacier-formed natural lakes in Grant County, perfect for swimming, boating, fishing, canoeing, and kayaking. The average monthly Fahrenheit temperatures range from the low 20's in the winter to the mid-70's in the summer.

After moving to Hancock Lake, Clarence took some time off before seeking new employment opportunities. He tackled some honey-do list items, repainted a few walls, installed a pier, and acquainted himself with the area. He purchased a used pontoon boat a week after moving to the lake. Clarence enjoyed fishing for bluegills, crappie, and bass off of his new pier and from the pontoon boat. Jean did not take time off from her new position. Her first day was the second day after they moved into their new home.

Clarence researched law enforcement employment opportunities in the area and found them to be limited. There was a small Sheriff's Department that served Grant County. The town of Wayne was also served by their own smaller police department, as were several other local communities in the county. There was an Ohio State Highway Patrol sub-district post in Wayne. The Ohio State Highway Patrol is a division of the Ohio Department of Public Safety.

Several weeks after beginning his job search, Clarence decided to apply for the lead detective's position, which had become available at the Grant County Sheriff's Department in Wayne, Ohio. He was pleasantly surprised when he received a call from the Sheriff's office requesting that he come in for an interview. It seemed there was more emphasis being placed in the Sheriff's Departments Detective Bureau than in the past. Crime was on the uptick and the community leaders thought it was time to address the increased need within the Sheriff's Department.

Clarence would take a serious cut in pay, if he accepted the position of Captain in the Detective Bureau for the Grant County Sheriff's Department. But living in rural Ohio was far less expensive than living in Chicago, and with Jean's increase in pay, Clarence knew they could afford the cut.

The Grant County Sheriff, Roger Jackson, offered the job to Clarence after a second interview. Clarence began working at the Sheriff's Department on Monday, October 10, 1988. Jackson appointed Moore as the lead investigator for the county because of his excellent record and experience as a veteran detective in the Chicago Police Department.

Clarence anticipated and was looking forward to a slower pace in Ohio compared to his former position in Chicago. And, he was correct. He spent the first few weeks learning the departmental procedures, getting to know personnel in the Sheriff's Department and in the County Prosecutor's office, and being given driving tours of the county. Clarence also spent time familiarizing himself with Ohio criminal law. The newly appointed Captain was shown the unsolved case files still under investigation. There were only a few such files and they were considered on-going investigations. The cases that were in the in-active status filing cabinet were turned over to the Ohio State Highway Patrol unsolved crime unit on an as needed basis.

Moore's partner and subordinate, Sergeant Randy T. Chilcott, was originally from Indiana. He was born and raised in Akron, Indiana on a farm. Chilcott was a shorter version of Moore at five-foot nine-inches tall, but he was lean and muscular. He weighed about one hundred forty-five pounds soaking wet. His cheeks were covered with patches of bright red rosacea. His hair color was light brown. Chilcott was eight years younger than Moore. He joined the Grant County Sheriff's Department five years after graduating high school.

Chilcott's girlfriend, Monica Kerlin was twenty-six-years-old and of Appalachian descent. She had perky breasts, wore loose fitting tops, tight jeans and high heels. She didn't wear a bra. That's what initially interested Chilcott in her, when he first encountered her as a waitress at a local truck-stop. Monica was thin, brunette, and not particularly attractive. She lived with Chilcott in his twenty-five-year-old modest aluminum-sided ranch home located in Wayne. Originally, the house was approximately 1,250 square feet, but sometime later, a 250 square foot master bedroom was added behind the two-car garage. The house was L-shaped with a basement and the home appeared properly kept, at least from the street. They were contemplating marriage.

Chilcott started out on the Sheriff's Department as a radio dispatcher before he was promoted to a full-time position as a patrol officer. After serving as a patrol officer for several years, he was promoted to Sergeant and temporarily put in charge of the Detective Bureau to fill an unexpected vacancy. As a five-year veteran of the Grant County Sheriff's Department, Chilcott was familiar with Ohio law enforcement procedures and statutes.

After Moore was hired at the rank of captain and appointed lead investigator for the Detective Bureau, Chilcott accepted the demotion without any apparent resentment. He knew his appointment as lead investigator was temporary. Chilcott had the general policing skills and knowledge, but not much experience as an investigator. He filled the role well enough to maintain the status quo, which allowed the Sheriff time to find and hire a suitable replacement for the former lead investigator, Captain Jacobs.

While vacationing in Florida, Captain Tom Jacobs and his wife were killed in a freak automobile accident on Interstate 75-N heading home. Moore appreciated Chilcott's gracious attitude and willingness to work with him, even though he had replaced Chilcott as lead investigator.

Former, Chicago Police Detective Clarence J. Moore was of English descent from the area known as Cheshire in Great Britain. His family immigrated to the United States in the mid 1800's. He was six-feet two-inches tall, lanky with mousy brown hair and eyes. His facial features were small and soft. Moore's skin tone was pale-white and he had some facial scaring from childhood battles on the basketball court. Jean thought he was handsome, particularly in uniform.

Brits are known for their dry sense of humor, serious nature, and love of tea. Clarence was no exception, even though his family's British accent and mannerisms had disappeared. He was an assimilated American in every respect.

Moore was very proud that his father served as a Chicago, Illinois policeman; so much so, that he followed in his father's footsteps by joining the department in 1973. He grew up in one of the best places in Illinois to live, the Edgewater section, a lakefront community on the North Side of Chicago, Illinois. Edgewater is six miles north of the Loop. Most of the families who lived there when Clarence was growing up rented their homes. Edgewater, then and now, has a dense urban feel. There are a lot of bars, restaurants, coffee shops, and parks.

Clarence J. Moore was born at Edgewater Medical Center in 1952 to Bessie and Nathan Moore. Nathan walked a beat for the Chicago Police Department in several precincts on the north side of the city. Since he wasn't Irish, his advancement possibilities were limited. Bessie was a high school English teacher. Nathan was killed in the line of duty three years after Clarence was born. Bessie remained single and never remarried. She raised Clarence the best she could. He grew up a normal kid, got good grades in school, and played shooting guard for Senn High School in Edgewater. During the summer he played on a team called 'The Breeze' in a Chicago basketball summer intramural league.

When faced with the decision to go to college or join the United States military in 1970, Clarence chose the Army. He enlisted after graduating from Senn High School. The Army seemed to be the answer for motivating and harnessing his behavior and for developing a work ethic and talent. After graduation from basic training, Clarence applied and received admittance into the military police training program. No doubt, the fact that Clarence was the son of a fatally injured police officer helped him to get the placement. He served three years in the United States Army attached to a criminal investigative unit. Clarence considered a career in the military police, but decided against it and was honorably discharged as an E-4 after completing his three-year enlistment.

After leaving the Army, Clarence applied and was accepted into the Chicago, Illinois Basic Metropolitan Recruit Program, which provides basic training for all law enforcement agencies in Illinois. The Chicago Police Department is the second largest municipal police force in the United States. The New York City Police Department is the largest. Over the years, Detective Moore earned the respect of his supervisors and fellow officers within the Detective Bureau by solving many crimes in several different Chicago precincts.

Working in the Grant County Sheriff's Department was a real change from being a detective on the Chicago Police Department. In Chicago, crime was usually violent. Clarence's cases included homicide, murder, assault, manslaughter, sexual assault, rape, robbery, endangerment, kidnapping, extortion, and harassment. The Windy City's non-violent crime list included bribery, prostitution, fraud, white collar crimes, arson, embezzlement, receipt of stolen goods, alcohol/drug related crimes, gambling, and racketeering.

Crime in Grant County was mostly limited to traffic violations, alcohol/drug related crime, robbery, burglary, aggravated assault, larceny theft, motor vehicle theft, manslaughter, and in rare cases rape and murder. The emergence of the various automotive accessory manufacturing companies in the Grant county area attracted workers from outside the county and state. Tourism also brought many people to the area from all around the nation. Sometimes the tourists and recently-settled workers turned out to be less than model citizens and trouble would ensue. That's when the police are needed. The mission of the Grant County Sheriff's Department was and is to preserve the peace by protecting all persons and property within the premises under control of the Judiciary and all states facilities for the citizens of Grant County.

Moore's shift started at eight a.m. and ended at five p.m. Chilcott usually arrived at the Sheriff's Department at 7 a.m. He claimed he couldn't sleep. Moore normally was there at seven-thirty a.m. A cup of hot tea was a priority for him before he started his work day. Moore's normal work days consisted of managing the Bureau, supervising Chilcott, and another patrol officer, who occasionally helped with the investigations. Moore spent his typical mornings reviewing the recent arrests and studying the case reports. He looked for similarities to other crimes that had been committed, but were unsolved. As needed, he, Chilcott, and sometimes the other patrol officer shared by the Detective Bureau would leave the office to investigate any reported crimes from the prior day to look for clues on unsolved cases.

On the morning of Tuesday, December 20, 1988, Moore was in the office early to take care of some needed paperwork. Jean was already on the road, headed for a store she managed in the Detroit area. Moore got up early and arrived at the Sheriff's Department a little after 5:15 a.m. He was drinking a cup of tea, when he received a call from the police dispatcher that there was a frantic caller who reported a homicide on the west side of the county.

Moore immediately called Chilcott at home and told him to get his clothes on and get to the Sheriff's

Department pronto. Moore told him to plan on working a possible homicide investigation. Eight minutes later, Chilcott arrived and met up with Moore and two on-duty patrol officers, who would accompany them to the Jacob Miller residence to help work the case. Chilcott informed the team that the Miller family was probably Old Order Amish, judging from their name and address.

During their drive to the crime scene, Chilcott informed Moore that, "The leaders of the Amish communities, the Bishops, Ministers, and Deacons, generally prefer to deal with bad behavior by their members within the confines of the church. They usually accomplish that with corporal punishment or temporary or permanent excommunication from the church. Our judicial system is often circumvented from prosecuting criminals who are members of the Amish community. The Amish believe in the principles of repentance before the church community and then forgiveness, for matters involving crime. They live by God's rules instead of man's."

Moore didn't fully understand the significance of Chilcott's statement, but he soon would. He would come to understand the Amish were different from the people he normally dealt with in Chicago.

"Very interesting people aren't they," Moore replied.

"Yes, the Amish are unique. You have no idea how much," Chilcott said with a grin.

"How much farther?" Moore asked.

"In about five more minutes we'll be there."

"You really know your way around the county," Moore

commented. “Have you been at the Millers residence before?”

“No, but I have a general idea where they live,” Chilcott said.

Moore thought, I’m impressed with Chilcott’s knowledge about the county roads. It sometimes feels to me as if they are crisscrossing the Grant County area without any logical design.

Chapter 2

Winters in northern Ohio are normally cold, snowy, and life seems dreary compared to the other three seasons. When the temperature drops to below freezing, living seems to become more fragile. Ice covered roadways, sidewalks, and driveways are slick and hazardous. The lack of sun and seeing overcast clouds, day after day, wear on a person's emotions, attitude, and behavior.

Those are some of the thoughts that might have been going through Jonathan Miller's mind at 4:30 a.m. as he faced the elements to feed his livestock. On that early Tuesday morning, he noted the light snow blowing in the yard, the driveway, and across the barren corn field. It was cold and dark outside. He carried a kerosene lantern to light his way. The light glistened on the snow flakes and reminded Jonathan of how beautiful winter was during a snowfall. Jonathan wore a heavy coat, broadfall pants, a plain-colored shirt, and work boots.

As a God-fearing baptized Christian and member of the Old Order Amish faith, Jonathan was thankful for what the Lord provided for him. Sustenance, forgiveness of his sins, happiness, and the assurance of a blessed life in the hereafter. He was almost a carbon copy of his father Jacob, except Jacob weighed two-hundred ten pounds and Jonathan weighed one-hundred eighty. Both men's hair and eyes were brown. Jonathan was not as stocky as Jacob, but they were the same height at five-foot eleven. As an unmarried Amish man, Jonathan could not grow his beard without shaving. But since Jacob was married wearing a beard was allowed. According to Amish tradition, wearing a beard shows you are a man of God. Jacob was proud of his eldest boy and gave him authority over the family in his absence.

Jonathan Miller was one of six sons born to Jacob and Sarah Miller. Jacob Miller's family roots were in Switzerland. Miller's forefathers moved from Europe in the early 18th century to the United States. They settled in Pennsylvania and then moved to Ohio in the late 1800's. As Old Order Amish the Millers attended Anabaptist services regularly with their eleven children. They had six boys and five girls. Jonathan was the oldest at nineteen.

The 85-acre Jacob Miller farm was located in northwestern Ohio's Amish country. The farm house was set back one-hundred feet from one of the main county roads leading to Wayne, Ohio from the west side of Grant County. The barn, implement building, workshop, and large out-building filled with chickens, were situated behind the farm house. There were several grain silos near the barn. All the wooden structures were painted white. The corrugated steel silos were unpainted. The remains of a dormant vegetable and flower garden were on the left side of the front yard, if one was facing the farm house. A small stand of maple trees occupied the other side of the front lawn. The maple trees provided maple syrup for the family's personal consumption. Mature pine trees lined the west and east perimeters of the land. Jacob planted the pines years earlier as a protective barrier against harsh winds and blowing snow.

The northwestern part of Ohio contains several concentrations of Amish people living in the United States. There are currently 342,000 Amish in the United States and their population is growing rapidly. The church member retention rate is eighty percent. Outside the City of Wayne and in Grant County there are several church districts or individual congregations where the Amish worship. Each congregation is comprised of around 30 families and their worship services are conducted in the members' homes on a rotating basis. There are close to a dozen or so Old Order Amish affiliations throughout the United States. The Old Order Amish have settled in about 20 states.

When Jonathan arrived at the barn door and opened it, he expected to hear the familiar sounds of hungry animals waiting impatiently for their morning meal. There were Belgian work horses, buggy horses, Shetland ponies, a dozen Holstein steers, and a few lambs to feed. Each was fed varying combinations of ground corn and oats, and hay, along with some vitamins and minerals. The chickens were housed in a large outbuilding adjacent to the barn. The laying hens provided the Millers with a stable income. That, coupled with their crop sales, the Millers were able to afford a reasonably good existence.

The majority of the hay bales were stored in the hay loft, in the upper level of the barn. The horses were on the main level. Steers and lambs had access to the lower level of the barn. Normally, the animals were overly enthusiastic to see Jonathan at feeding time. But Jonathan sensed some anxiety or a strange fervor in their behavior as he entered the barn. However, his initial concern subsided when he began to feed the horses. As he worked his way to the back through the multi-level barn, where several bales of hay were stacked up below the hayloft on the main floor, all of a sudden, his eyes opened wide in surprise. In front of a bale of hay, a body lay on top of a horse blanket on the floor. Blood was everywhere on the blanket and the floor.

Jonathan cautiously approached the scene and looked at the back side of a young Amish girl. There was a large wound on the back of her head. She was covered in blood. He carefully flipped the body over and to his astonishment discovered it was his oldest sister Rachael. She was lying there in her home-made dress and winter coat. The coat was open and the dress partially unsnapped. The girl was covered with blood, dirt, and hay. Her breasts were partially exposed, even though her white brassier was not unhooked. Her white underpants were pulled down around her ankles. Her pubic hair and privates were visible.

Jonathan stared briefly at her body, finding it difficult to view the horrible after-effects of an apparent attack. His sister was obviously a victim. He thought she was probably dead, but he felt her bluish skin to be sure. Her skin was stone cold and ice particles had formed on her lips, nose, and eyes. For a moment the terrible sight left Jonathan in a catatonic state. It felt like a creepy, surrealistic dream.

When he awoke and realized it wasn't a dream, Jonathan started to panic. But he quickly came to his senses again, turned, and ran toward the house. Jonathan screamed for his father to come out.

Moments later, father and son rushed back to the barn. Jacob Miller was shocked to see Rachael's dead body lying on the ground. Trailing not far behind the two men was Rachael's mother, Sarah. Jacob tried to shield his wife from going to Rachael's lifeless body but to no avail. Sarah dropped to the ground, covered her daughter's privates, and held her in her arms. Slowly, she began to whimper and then sob uncontrollably as she cradled Rachael's corpse.

One by one, the rest of the siblings joined the family in the barn. At first, they stood in shock looking at their deceased sister lying on the ground in front of them. Jonathan stood next to his parents and watched as the heartrending emotions poured out of his parents and siblings. He was still in a state of shock and his mouth hung wide open. There was fear in his eyes as he looked at his dead sister and around the barn. Thankfully, there was no one in the barn, except the family.

After about five minutes of grieving Jacob arose and instructed Jonathan to hitch a horse up to their buggy. Jacob told him to go to the closest "English" neighbor with a telephone and call the authorities for help. The elder Miller said to his son, "I will stay with Rachael and the family until the police arrive."

After what seemed like an eternity, the Millers finally heard the sounds of police sirens coming toward them from off in the distance. The closer the police cruisers got, the louder the sirens became. Jonathan waited patiently for them to arrive at the entrance to the driveway. When the police vehicles arrived, the sirens were turned off. Jonathan directed the police to drive back to the barn.

A small entourage of policemen entered the barn, looked over the crime scene, and then began their normal investigation procedures. Jacob Miller ordered his family to leave the barn and go back inside the house to allow the Sheriff's deputies to do their work. One of the policemen was wearing a white shirt with a blue tie. He wore a heavy, dark overcoat with a woolen scarf and cap. He appeared to be in charge. Miller watched as the detective quickly reminded the officers to put on their rubber gloves before examining the crime scene. After he finished looking over the crime scene, Captain Moore said to the other officers, "The weapon, which appears to have caused her death is that big, long spike, which is sticking out of the post about three inches. He pointed to the spike which was driven into the post about four-feet off the barn floor. The post with the protruding spike was just a few feet away from where the body lay. There was dried blood on the spike, the post, the corpse, the blanket, and the hay covering the ground between the body and the post.

After several more minutes of inspecting the premises, the detective introduced himself to the Amish man standing quietly in the corner of the barn still gazing at the body. He approached the Amish man, removed his right rubber glove, extended his hand, and said, "Mr. Miller, I am Captain Moore with the Grant County Sheriff's Department. I'll be handling the investigation. He flashed his badge and said, “Do you mind if I ask you several questions?”

The elder Miller limply shook the detective’s hand and said in a melancholy tone, “Glad to meet you, officer. I will answer whatever questions you have.”

“Thank you,” said Moore. “I presume the deceased girl is your daughter.”

Miller nodded in acknowledgement.

“Are you sure you’re up for a few questions, Mr. Miller?” Moore asked again.

“Yes, I think so officer,” Miller replied.

“I will try to be as quick as possible with my questioning so you can get back to your family.”

Miller’s voice was strained, but he acknowledged softly that, “She was my oldest girl and just turned fifteen.”

Moore saw a few tears forming in the father’s eyes and dripping down his cheeks as he spoke. “I’m very sorry. Normally, it’s a nice age to be,” said Detective Moore. He opened a small pad of paper and took out the pen in his pocket. He jotted some information on the pad. “First of all, it appears your daughter was killed by the spike on that post.” He turned and pointed to the metal spike sticking out of the post. “I believe the back of her head was pierced by the spike. It could be accidental or was done by someone on purpose. The spike is most likely the cause of death, but we will let the coroner decide for sure. How do you spell your daughter’s full name, and what was her date of birth?”

Miller spelled her full name and provided her date of birth for the detective. Moore recorded the information on the pad and said "Thank you."

Miller nodded in acknowledgement.

"When was the body found?"

"My son, Jonathan, found her body this morning at 4:30 a.m."

"What brought him to the barn?"

"His daily chores include feeding the livestock every morning."

The detective nodded and scribbled another bit of information on the pad. "I see," he said. Moore noted Jacob Miller wore a heavy coat, home-made pants with suspenders, a light blue-colored shirt, and work shoes. He had a large build and a small belly that hung over his pants. However, he looked to be stout and strong. His finger nails were dirty and his hands were rough and cracked. Moore looked up at Miller and said, "I'd say your daughter has been dead for maybe eight to ten hours."

"How can you be sure of that?" asked Miller with a furrowed brow.

"From experience with other cases."

"I see," replied the Amish man.

"Did you see Rachael leave the house last evening?"

"No. I did not pay much attention to her activities last night. I was tired and dozed off in my recliner reading the Good Book," he said. "She obviously went outside, but I did not see her."

"Judging from the crime scene, I'd say this incident happened sometime early last evening. Looking at the condition of her body and the coagulation of blood, I'd say this occurred sometime between 8:00 p.m. and 10:00 p.m. last night."

"Yes, maybe so, but I didn't hear or see anything out of the ordinary. We go to bed around 9:00 p.m."

"Did she have any visitors last evening that you are aware of, Mr. Miller?"

"No, I'm not aware of Rachael having any guests."

"Well, obviously someone else was probably with her," Detective Moore replied with a slight hint of sarcasm.

"Yes, I guess you're right. Someone must have been in the barn with her," Miller replied.

"Did Rachael have any enemies that you know of?"

"Detective, she is a fifteen-year-old girl. Who could have anything against her?" Miller asked in amazement at the suggestion. Several tear drops appeared in his eyes again, but he quickly regained his composure.

"Does she have a boyfriend?"

"She has lots of friends, boys and girls. Everyone seemed to like Rachael," Miller claimed.

"Was there anyone special?"

"Not that I'm aware of."

"Thanks for your cooperation, Mr. Miller. I don't have

any more questions for you right now. Although, I would like to interview your family tomorrow, if possible."

"Whatever questions you have for me or a member of my family, I will answer them for you," Miller stated emphatically, yet politely.

"Oh, it would be better if I could speak to them directly," Moore replied equally politely but firmly. He wondered whether it was an Amish custom for the father to speak for the family. He didn't want to bother the grieving family needlessly, but he also wanted to follow proper procedures on his first probable homicide case in the new job.

"No, I will speak for the family," Miller said firmly.

"Alright," Moore conceded. He did not want to anger the Amish man, since he needed his cooperation. "I've notified a Grant county funeral home and they will be arriving shortly to take Rachael to the County Morgue for processing. Is that alright with you?"

"What is processing?" Miller asked sounding confused.

"Processing is a term used when a coroner or doctor looks for clues on a deceased victim's body to help solve the crime."

"Okay, I understand. But just so you understand, Rachael will need to be embalmed professionally and then returned to our home for viewing as soon as possible. According to Amish tradition, burials are to be done within three days from the death. That does not give us much time."

“I’m sure the Grant County Coroner will do his best to accommodate your church rules. When the mortician arrives, I’ll come and get you so you can make your arrangements with him. Is that alright with you, Mr. Miller? Also, please express my condolences to Mrs. Miller and your family.”

“Yes. Thank you, officer, for your kindness and concern,” Miller said as he turned to rejoin his family in the farm house. Moore noted how disheartened Miller looked as the father of the dead girl walked slowly out of the barn.

After Miller was out of the barn Moore conferred with the other investigators, who were looking for potential clues as to the perpetrator of the crime. Chilcott reported that he saw some buggy tracks on the road leading into the property, and the tracks appeared to be leaving and returning to the property. Moore wondered, who made those tracks. There was no sign of a violent struggle inside the barn.

There was a small flashlight on the ground several feet from the body. *Hopefully, they will be able to get prints from the flashlight*, Moore thought. A medium-size mostly empty paper cup, which smelled like it contained a combination of alcohol and a soft drink, was found near the front of the barn. The straw and the lid were on the ground next to the cup. Moore wondered, whether the person who disposed of the cup was the killer of the Amish girl. He could have dropped the cup as he fled the crime scene. Of course, the person who held the cup might not be connected to the crime. He might have been driving by the farm and threw it out the window of his vehicle. If the later was true, the cup could have been blown toward the barn by gusting winds. Moore figured there would be DNA evidence on the cup and the straw. If there was DNA found, that information could be invaluable in helping to solve the crime. At the moment, nothing else of interest was found at the crime scene.

When investigating a crime scene, the normal procedure for the police is to gather as much evidence as possible. Usually it includes lifting latent finger prints from the surfaces in or around the crime scene. But any possible latent prints on the rough wooden surfaces, inside or outside the barn, could not be lifted due to the texture of the wood. However, there were prints on some of the smoother surfaces of lumber inside the barn. The barn door was not locked and the windows were smeared with dirt. Moore looked through the windows and noted that it was difficult to see through the grime. He didn't see any foot prints that led from the county road to the barn and back. Detective Moore realized that the blowing snow might have covered up older prints to and from the barn. The only visible foot prints came from the farm house to the barn and back. As the light snow continued to fall and be blown about the property, even that evidence was going to quickly disappear. There was a dirt access road next to the barn leading into the corn field. The ground was mostly frozen, but there was a partial tire print taken from the access road. In addition, Moore assumed the body had been moved to some extent by the family, so the crime scene was altered by the time the investigators arrived.

Moore hoped that an autopsy might give them either a

semen sample, a DNA sample, or that a toxicology report might reveal ingested drugs, or something concrete to help them solve the case. The detective even considered the possibility that the girl might have gone to the barn to pleasure herself and accidentally fell backwards as she got up to return to the house. There was no apparent bruising on the victims face. If there was a struggle it was not evident, but the coroner would examine the body more thoroughly for bruising and other physical clues.

After meeting with Jacob Miller, Detective Moore realized policing in Grant County was going to be quite different than in Cook County, Illinois. He lacked experience in dealing with the Amish and had little or no understanding of the Amish culture. Moore would soon discover the Amish to be a close-knit society made up of people who rarely involve the authorities and have a different view of the traditional criminal justice system than ordinary citizens the Amish refer to as the "English." It appeared to Moore that this case was going to be difficult to unravel.

Chapter 3

Inside the barn, Captain Moore was concluding his over four-hour investigation of the crime scene, when he heard the purring sound of an automobile engine in the driveway. He looked out the barn window and saw a black hearse stopped next to the police cars. He looked at his watch. It was 9:50 a.m. He assumed it was the mortician from Wayne, Ohio. *Apparently, he's finally arrived,* Moore thought. Sunshine was partially breaking through the snow clouds and the fallen snow glistened from the sun light.

Sitting in the hearse were two men. The sign on the driver's side door read, "Blair-Samuels Funeral Home". The driver exited the vehicle while the passenger remained inside. The man wore a black hat and a dark overcoat. He pulled on his gloves as he walked to the barn and slid open the barn door.

An older man of small stature entered the barn just as the police investigation was about to conclude. The Deputy Sheriffs' were putting away their gear and wrapping things up. Meanwhile, Moore stood gazing at the increasingly heavy snowfall and listening to the howling wind. He realized it would not take very long for the snow to pile up against the buildings and cover the ground. Moore knew this was not a good development for their investigation. Foot prints and buggy tracks would be lost forever. *Thank God for photographs*, Moore thought. He imagined trying to maintain the integrity of the crime scene at a working farm would be next to impossible.

As Moore continued to look out the window, he thought about the progress of the investigation, thus far. They examined the corpse, collected several items of potential evidence, obtained some latent fingerprints, photographed the victim, and photographed the crime scene inside and outside of the barn. He also preliminarily interviewed Jacob Miller, the father of the deceased girl. He wanted to interview the rest of the family in spite of the insistence of Mr. Miller that he would "speak for the family".

Moore wondered what the prosecutor would say about Mr. Miller's announcement. *Did Miller want to hinder the investigation? Why would he want to do that? Could Jacob Miller be the perpetrator of the crime? Should he Mirandize Miller at the time of his formal interrogation?* He'd spoken briefly with Miller in the barn and Moore didn't think Miller fit the profile of a killer. But who knows for sure. So far, he did not have all the facts and Miller was not a suspect. So, he decided he would not Mirandize Miller during the course of the interrogation. However, if there was any evidence revealed during the interview that seemed to indicate Miller might be guilty of the crime, he would immediately give him the Maranda warning. So, the prosecution would be able to use any evidence Miller gave up, if he agreed to allow the interrogation to continue.

When Moore turned away from the window to greet the mortician, he observed the older, gray-haired man looking down at the corpse. “It’s a shame, isn’t it? The girl was only fifteen-years-old,” Moore said to the mortician.

The mortician turned and looked directly into Moore’s eyes and said, “Yes, it’s truly a shame. Unfortunately, we humans do not always treat each other very well.” Extending his hand to the detective, the mortician said, “I’m Franklin Blair, with the Blair-Samuels Funeral Home in Wayne.”

Moore shook his hand and said, “Good morning. I’m Captain Moore with the Grant County Sheriff’s Department’s Detective Bureau. Unfortunately, we are often faced with dealing with man’s inhumanity to man, in our professions. I’m sure you’d agree.”

“Sad, but true,” Blair said nodding his head in agreement with the officer. I’ve worked with the Grant County authorities for years, but we’ve never met before.” Blair commented as he gave Moore a look over.

“That’s because I am new to this police department,” Moore proclaimed. “Previously, I worked as a detective for fifteen years on the Chicago Police Department.”

“Interesting, I’m certain that you’ve seen plenty of homicides in the past, Captain.”

“Yes. Unfortunately, I have. But you can never really get used to seeing a murder victim and particularly this young. It’s very hard and over time it takes a toll on you. That is unless, you’re a heartless person or a psychopath,”

Moore replied matter-of-factly.

"I agree," said Blair somberly. "Are you finished examining the body detective?"

"I think so. Oh, before I forget, you need to talk to Mr. Miller about embalming his daughter. He's waiting inside the house to talk to you."

"That's fine, I'll go meet with him when we're finished here," the undertaker said. "I'll have my assistant collect the body shortly. Would one of your officers be able to help secure her body on the gurney?"

"Sure, no problem. Glad to help."

"If I could trouble you for one more thing before I leave, it would be appreciated."

"What do you need, Mr. Blair?" Moore asked.

"Could you please give me the name of the deceased and her date of birth? I also need to have her parents' names for the record."

Moore provided the information to the mortician, who nodded in appreciation and thanked him with a smile. Before leaving the barn, Blair thanked Moore once again for his assistance and walked out of the barn to the farm house to meet with Mr. and Mrs. Jacob Miller.

Captain Moore thought to himself, *most undertakers look and act very much the same. Franklin Blair is no exception. He was polite, appropriately attired, sincere, and solemn.* Moore wondered, whether he could work with deceased people and their relatives, day in and day out. He concluded it was a job he wouldn't want, even though it was necessary and lucrative.

Franklin Blair walked up to the farm house and knocked on the back door. He identified himself to the Millers and expressed his condolences. They invited Blair inside their home and to sit down to talk at the kitchen table. Mr. Miller informed Blair that he wanted his daughter Rachael to be properly embalmed and then returned to their home for viewing as soon as possible.

Blair assured the Millers he would do a good job of preparing her for the funeral service and returning her back to them as soon as possible. However, he said, "I am employed by the Grant County Coroner's office to first deliver your child to the County Morgue, which is located in the basement of the Grant County Community Hospital. Once at the morgue, an autopsy will be performed on her," explained Blair. "Just so you understand, I can't embalm her until after the autopsy is completed and Rachael's body is released to me by the Coroner."

The couple looked at each other with puzzled looks on their faces and said, "Why is an autopsy necessary?"

Blair replied plainly, "Any time there is a questionable death reported to the authorities about a minor, the incident by law must be investigated. Most of the time the authorities will do an autopsy to determine the cause of death."

"Will we be required to pay for Rachael's delivery to the morgue and the autopsy?" asked the Amish man directly.

The mortician responded, "No, but you will be charged

for the embalming procedure and for my picking-up and delivering your loved one back to your home."

"Alright, I see," Miller said. "When will she be returned to us so we can schedule the viewing, funeral, and burial? Our preference is to bury Rachael three days from her death."

"I'm aware of your traditions, but it is not up to me. The County Coroner will make that decision. I'm sure he will try to expedite the processing."

"Yes, I hope so," Miller said.

"Am I to assume that you will provide a coffin?" Blair inquired.

"Yes, my cousin is a cabinet maker and he'll make the coffin. I'll drop it off to you in a couple of days. Will that be soon enough?"

"That should be fine," the mortician said. "I'll also need to have an appropriate dress for her to wear in the coffin."

"I'll have Jacob bring a freshly washed dress, cap, and apron, when he brings the coffin," Mrs. Miller proclaimed.

"That will be fine. I'll make sure she looks very nice for the funeral."

"We've heard good things about your funeral home, Mr. Blair," Miller added. "I'm sure you will do a good job."

"Thank you," Blair replied with a smile. "We always try to do our best for our patrons. One more thing, I'll be happy to help you with a death notice for the newspaper. It's a free service and we will deliver it to the newspaper once the time-table is known."

"Thank you," the Amish man said. "Would you like our family information now?"

"Yes, that would be fine," Blair said. He pulled out a single page form from inside his overcoat pocket and began helping the couple fill it out. When it was completed, he placed the form back into his coat pocket.

"We are about ready to take Rachael's body to the morgue. Would you like to see her one more time before we leave," Blair offered sympathetically.

"That's very nice, but I don't think so," Miller said while looking at his wife. Sarah, who nodded her approval of his decision. "We've seen enough," Miller said glumly.

"That will be fine," Blair responded. "If you have any questions or concerns the funeral home's address and phone number are on this business card. I'm so sorry about your loss." The mortician handed his card to Miller, got up, and shook Miller's hand. He nodded respectfully to Mrs. Miller, shook her hand, and departed the home.

A few minutes later, Detective Moore knocked on the Millers' back door. Miller opened the door and invited him to come inside. Moore could smell the distinct odor of a wood burning stove. He saw the stove, which was located in the corner of the kitchen. It appeared to be filled with wood and coal. Through the front access cover, he could see a blazing fire inside. "Do you mind if I warm my hands?" Moore asked. "It was very cold in the barn," he commented.

"Please, go and get warm," Mrs. Miller insisted. "Can I get you some coffee, tea or something else to drink," she asked politely.

"Yes, thank you. Tea would be nice."

After several minutes of standing by the stove warming himself up, Miller invited the detective to take a seat at the kitchen table. The Amish man said to Moore, "It's been a rough day for all of us, hasn't it?"

"Yes, it surely has," Moore admitted as he casually glanced around the inside of the farm house while sipping the hot tea. He noticed a large dining area, a large living room with a heater probably run by propane from the tank outside near the back of the house. He assumed the bedrooms were on the main and second floors of the home.

Turning his attention back to the Millers, he asked, "Did you get things handled with Mr. Blair?"

"Yes, we did," Mrs. Miller responded, which surprised Moore, since her husband had answered all previous questions pertaining to the death of their daughter. "He was very nice to us. He explained the need for an autopsy, which I think you referred to as processing to my husband."

"Yes, I've been told by many people that saying processing is preferred over using the technical term, autopsy. It sounds less disturbing."

"No need to discuss things like that in too much detail, I suppose," Mr. Miller said.

Moore told the Millers that their initial phase of the police investigation was concluded for the day, but that he would be back to ask some more questions the following day.

The elder Miller assured the detective that he would be happy to cooperate with the police investigation. He commented, "I want to put this matter behind our family as quickly as possible."

Finding the comment somewhat unusual," Moore replied, "I intend to find out what happened to Rachael and hold someone responsible for her death. But you understand those things will take time."

Miller responded, "Yes, I imagine that they will. But, remember detective, whatever happened to Rachael was God's will. There will be a day of reckoning for the person who took our daughter's life. We can be sure of it."

"I totally agree, Mr. Miller." Although Moore was not currently connected to a specific religion or attended church regularly, he was raised Presbyterian and believed in God. Moore wondered what differences existed between the Anabaptist and the Presbyterian faiths. He knew it would be wise for him to do some research on the Anabaptist church in order for him to better understand the Amish.

As Detective Moore got up to leave, he thanked Mrs. Miller for the tea and expressed his condolences to both the elder Millers. He noticed the other family members remained quiet and kept themselves seated in the living room during the conversation.

Prior to going to the farm house to talk to the Millers, Moore had released the two on-duty Sheriff's deputies to return to their normal routines. They were already gone by the time he got back to the squad car. Sergeant Chilcott was waiting patiently for Moore to return to the unmarked vehicle. After leaving the barn, Chilcott started the vehicle and turned up the heat. When Moore got back into the car, he was pleased to find the interior was warm and comfortable. "Thank you for all your help today, Randy," Moore said.

"No problem, Captain. I loaded up the equipment and evidence. It's safely stored in the trunk. We can stop by the morgue on the way back to the Sheriff's Department if you want to talk to the coroner," Chilcott suggested.

"No, I think I'll wait to meet the coroner and ask questions once the autopsy has been completed and the results are known. Let's get back to the office. I'd like to contact the sheriff and talk to him about how he wants me to proceed. I'd also like to check our records to determine if any family member has any history of violent behavior."

"I'll do it," Chilcott said as he put the car in gear and turned on to the county road leading back to Wayne. Chilcott continued, "I need to take the film to our photo lab to be developed. I think I got some pretty good shots. Although, you never know what you've got until you look at the pictures."

On the twenty-minute drive back to the Sheriff's Department, Moore looked over at Chilcott and said, "You know these people better than I do. What's your initial take on who might have done this thing?"

"Heck, I hate to say it, but I think someone in the family knows what really happened and they're keeping quiet. I suspect either the eldest son, Jonathan, or his father could be involved. What do you think, Captain?"

Moore was not totally surprised that Chilcott was willing to speculate about the guilt or innocence of someone without knowing all the facts. After all, Chilcott had received no formal training as a detective. But Moore was slightly disappointed with the officer's answer. He responded to Chilcott saying, "I think you could be on to something, but I think it's always wise to first review all the evidence before coming to a conclusion. In the end, it's really not up to either one of us to decide who is guilty or not. Our job is to collect evidence and the prosecuting attorney will make that determination by what he thinks he can prove in court. But, of course, you knew that, didn't you?

"Yes, of course I did," Chilcott said turning a little pink with embarrassment.

"*I doubt if he knew what the correct answer should have been, but at least he knows better now*," Moore thought, who was testing his young Sergeant as to his knowledge concerning police procedure and the law. *I think I'll wait to interview the Millers until after the services are concluded. It will give Mr. Miller time to think about letting me interview his family individually.*

Chapter 4

Franklin Blair pulled his 1985 Buick LeSabre black hearse into the back of the Grant County Community Hospital. When he arrived at the loading dock, he backed into the designated space at 10:45 a.m. Normally, they would have used the panel van to transport the body, but it was in the shop for repairs. He and his assistant Bill Nusbaum opened the rear door and removed the gurney from inside the hearse. They opened the overhead door and rolled the covered corpse strapped to the gurney into the lower-level of the hospital. Blair flipped on the light switch in the hallway and helped to guide the gurney toward the county morgue.

When they arrived at the morgue, the pathologist's assistant from the hospital staff unlocked the door and let the two men enter. Morgues contain stainless steel autopsy tables, equipment, and freezers. They are like any other surgical facility in hospitals, except they hold deceased patients and homicide victims. Like a lot of other places in the hospital, morgues have an antiseptic, dreary feel to them. Many morgues are not clearly labeled. If you were not actively looking for them, you would likely not realize the facilities were morgues.

"Good morning, Mr. Blair," Barney Yoder said as they entered the morgue. He flipped on the main light switches. "I was told you were bringing in a young Amish girl to us. How did she die?"

Recognizing the pathologists assistant, Blair responded, "The police are not sure yet, Barney. They will be relying on Dr. Peterson and the Coroner to help make that determination."

"Dr. Peterson and the Coroner have already been notified. I'm expecting them to be arriving shortly."

"Please make sure to let us know when the autopsy is completed. Bill and I need to get her ready for viewing as soon as possible," Blair said.

"I'll be sure you're called," Barney replied. "Let's place the body inside a freezer for the time being until they are ready to conduct their examination." Blair watched as Yoder and Nusbaum removed Rachael Miller's body from the gurney and placed it inside freezer #1.

About ten minutes later, Dr. William Peterson appeared in the morgue. Peterson interned at the University of Michigan Hospital in Ann Arbor, Michigan. He grew up in the Lake James area of Steuben County in Indiana. Peterson was thrilled when an opening became available for a staff pathologist position in Grant County. He came from a wealthy family and had no interest in accumulating any more wealth. He just wanted to practice his medical duties as close to Lake James as possible. Peterson was short, looked almost undernourished, although he wasn't, with blond hair and green eyes. He always wore funny colored bow-ties, enjoyed classical music, and was very intelligent. The Grant County Community Hospital was lucky to have such a high caliber physician as Peterson. He rarely saw patients. His main function was to help diagnose disease and illness and to recommend treatment. This was in addition to his responsibilities as the staff pathologist assigned to conduct autopsies.

Paul Smith had been the Grant County Coroner for almost sixteen years. He was in his final term in office. He had decided to retire on his sixty-sixth birthday. Smith was sixty-five years old. He attended college at Tri-State University in Auburn, Indiana and received a degree in business management. Smith owned and operated a hometown grocery store in Wayne, Ohio. He was six-foot four-inches tall and weighed approximately two-hundred sixty pounds. He loved to fish, hunt, eat, and he cared about people. He was not a medical doctor, so he relied on people like Dr. William Peterson to perform the autopsies.

When Smith arrived at the morgue, he wasn't surprised to see that Dr. Peterson was ready to start the procedure. Peterson wore a surgical gown, cap, mask, headlamp, and rubber gloves. His gear also included waterproof boots and an apron. "Good morning doctor," Smith said. "I'll be suited up and ready to go in five minutes."

"Sounds good to me," Dr. Peterson replied. "I've got a busy day planned and I'm supposed to meet my mother for dinner tonight." Peterson turned and said to the assistant, "Barney, please remove the body from the freezer and I'll help you place it on the examination table."

"Will do, Dr. Peterson."

Several minutes later, Smith arrived at the examination table and the forensic autopsy began. They first unzipped the black plastic covering to expose the corpse. Next, they removed all of the deceased girl's clothing including her shoes, socks, under garments, dress, and winter coat. Barney placed them off to the side for later examination. Her naked body was face up on the stainless-steel table. The coroner turned on the high intensity overhead light and started a small recording device. "Who do we have here today, Barney?" Smith asked routinely.

Barney handed the Sheriff's Department's homicide report to Smith. Barney said, "Blair-Samuels Funeral Home received this report after taking possession of the body from the Grant County Sheriff's Department earlier this morning."

Smith began to record the proceeding by stating that I, Paul Smith, Grant County Coroner, and Dr. William Peterson are conducting this autopsy on Tuesday, December 20, 1988 at 11:05 a.m. He read the police report directly into the microphone. "Grant County Sheriff's Department homicide report dated Tuesday, December 20, 1988. The deceased is Rachael Miller a fifteen-year-old Caucasian female, who lived on County Road W200S in Grant County, Ohio. She is approximately four-feet ten-inches tall with brown hair and brown eyes. Her parents are Jacob and Sarah Miller of the same address. When the body was discovered her dress was unsnapped and opened. Her underpants were around her ankles. In reviewing the evidence at the crime scene, it suggested that the homicide might also involve rape. There were no visible tattoos or markings found on her body and there was a large hole, a half inch in diameter, on the back of her skull at the top of her neck. The wound was believed to have been caused by either the deceased accidentally falling back into a protruding three-inch timber spike or she was purposely pushed into the spike. The spike was approximately four-feet high off the ground. The spike appeared to have been driven into a post on the main floor of the barn and extended approximately three-inches out of the post. The estimated time of death was sometime before ten p.m. on Monday, December 19, 1988. The girl was found by her nineteen-year-old brother, Jonathan Miller, the following Tuesday morning at 4:30 a.m. Her father, Mr. Jacob Miller, was interviewed, but there are no motives, witnesses, or suspects being pursued at this time. The other family members will be interviewed either tomorrow or early next week. The body was turned over to the Blair-Samuel's Funeral Home in Wayne, Ohio for delivery to the Grant County Morgue. The report is signed by Captain Clarence J. Moore of the Grant County Sheriff's Department Detective Bureau."

"Alright gentlemen, let us begin," Coroner Smith instructed. "Do you think we need to do a full forensic autopsy, since it's pretty certain what killed her from the police report, Dr. Peterson?"

"Yes, a forensic autopsy would be appropriate in this case, but I don't believe it would be necessary to conduct a complete forensic autopsy either. I think we should look into doing blood tests, urine analysis, and some tests related to a probable rape in this particular case. We also should examine the condition and the extent of damage done to the brain stem. In addition, we need to check her clothing for any DNA evidence."

"As you know Paul, normally we would remove all her organs including her brain. Then we'd weigh and measure them and study them to determine the cause of death. But in this case, I think it would be a waste of taxpayer funds. Don't you agree?" Peterson asked plainly.

"I agree, Doctor. Okay, we'll handle it as you see fit," Smith replied. "Barney, please hand me the camera. I need to take several pictures of the body." After shooting several photos, Smith checked the recording device to make sure it was turned on and working properly. He spoke into the microphone again saying, "First, let's check her height and weight, Doctor."

Dr. Peterson measured the corpse and said, "Four-foot ten-inches is correct. Her weight is slightly over one-hundred pounds. I'll draw several tubes of blood and we'll get a complete blood count and a comprehensive metabolic panel to determine the condition of the deceased at the time of her death. These tests should show any irregularities in her system." He grabbed the tubes, labeled them, indicated the tests he wanted conducted, and then drew several samples of blood. Peterson also collected a urine sample taken from her bladder. He handed the tubes and the urine sample to Barney and said, "Please, take these to the laboratory for testing. Make sure they test her urine for alcohol or drugs."

Due to the assumption by the detectives that she might have been raped. Dr. Peterson decided to do a pelvic exam.

He quickly discovered she had been bleeding from inside her uterus. He also found something that looked like fetal tissue still attached to the side wall of her uterus. Not surprisingly, Peterson determined that the tissue was part of an embryonic membrane still attached to the uterus. Something that was not uncommon following a miscarriage. He removed a small section of the tissue with a scalpel. He had noted that her hymen was torn, which could have been the result of sexual penetration, riding a bike, or wearing a tampon. However, she had obviously been pregnant sometime prior to her death and thus had been sexually active. "Let's check to see if there is any presence of sperm in her uterus," Peterson said to Smith. They searched inside her uterus, vagina, and outside on her vulva for any dried semen or active sperm. The team found none.

"Maybe she wasn't raped after all," Smith commented.

"I'll see if I can find any loose pubic hairs intertwined in her vulva area," Peterson said. After checking the area thoroughly, it appeared there was no foreign pubic hair on her body either. With no presence of sperm and no foreign pubic hairs on her body, Dr. Peterson was doubtful she had been raped.

The team examined her upper torso for bruising and redness. Smith noted there was some slight bruising on both shoulders and her face exhibited a small red abrasion on the left cheek. The team concluded the redness on her cheek could have been the result of the fall. The shoulder bruising could have been a result of another injury. The two men agreed that working around a farm could be dangerous at times.

When Barney returned from the laboratory a half-hour later, he said to Dr. Peterson, "They found no trace of drugs or alcohol in her urine sample. The other lab results look completely normal too." Both men were not surprised. They knew that Amish girls at her age are pretty sheltered kids. At sixteen, however, Amish are exposed to the phenomena of Rumspringa, and that's normally when problems arise.

Before flipping the girl over to examine her wound, Dr. Peterson said, "I'd like to do one more test. It could help us determine how far along she might have been in her pregnancy. I'm convinced she was in the first trimester, but I'm curious. I'd like to know what her Relaxin level was when she died." He drew another tube of blood, labeled it, and handed it to Barney. "Please, take this sample to the laboratory and ask them to do a Relaxin level test."

"What is Relaxin, Dr. Peterson?" Smith inquired. "I've never heard of it before."

"Relaxin is a hormone produced by the ovary and placenta during pregnancy. Usually, a female's level is moderate, but increases rapidly after she becomes pregnant. Relaxin relaxes the walls of the uterus by inhibiting contractions and it also prepares the lining of the uterus for pregnancy."

After Barney left the examination room, both Peterson and Smith turned the body over and were amazed when they saw the size of the hole near the lower base of the girl's skull. Smith took several more photographs of her backside and then got close-ups of the wound on the rear base of her skull. "The spike appears to have entered into the brain stem at least three inches, if not more," Peterson said after measuring the depth of the hole.

There was dried blood caked on and inside the wound. They cleaned the area thoroughly until they could see the extent of the damage. "Apparently, the spike made a hole the size of a dime at the top of her neck," Smith remarked.

"It looks like the spike was driven into the body as she went backwards," Peterson replied. "The result was the nail punctured her skin right under the base of her skull and was driven directly into her brain stem. This appears to be a life-ending injury."

"I see!" Smith said amazed at how much damage the spike caused.

"The brain stem is the lower part of the brain that's connected to the spinal cord. It is part of the central nervous system in the spinal column. Brain stems are responsible for regulating most of the body's automatic functions that are essential for life. They include your breathing, heartbeat, blood pressure, and swallowing. The brain stem also relays important information to and from the brain to the rest of the body. Once there is severe damage to the brain stem, death occurs. However, it is possible for someone to remain alive but unconscious for a time in a coma. But considering the severity of this injury, that would be very unlikely. Actually, it should be a blessing to her loved ones that she is not in the hospital existing in a vegetative state with the help of oxygen and on a ventilator. I'd say we can record the cause of death as severe damage to her brain stem," Peterson concluded.

Examining her backside, the team could not discover any further damage to her body or bruising. "Did someone take a look at her clothing?" Smith asked.

"Yes and no," Peterson replied. "I inspected her underpants for sperm samples and any foreign pubic hair. I found nothing foreign. The rest of the clothing was dirty, worn, and blood covered."

"How did I miss your examination of the panties?"

"I think that was when you went to the restroom."

"I guess you're right, but it didn't seem like I was gone that long to me."

"I should have waited for you before checking her underwear, Paul. Sorry!"

"No big deal, Doctor. Let's move on."

We should examine the blood samples on her clothing to make sure the blood belongs to her and not someone else," Dr. Peterson said.

"I'll scrape some samples from various blood spots on the jacket and make some slides. You can compare them on a microscope. I doubt if we're going to find someone else's blood, but you can check," Smith said. "What else do we need to examine?"

"We should look over the clothing and see if there are any body hairs or fiber samples that do not belong on the deceased clothes."

"Of course, we should," Smith agreed. After spending

approximately an hour inspecting her things, Dr. Peterson determined there was nothing unusual on the girl's clothing. Mostly, the items on her coat and clothing were dried mud, hay with traces of manure, blood, and her own dried skin on the collar of her winter coat.

"As far as I'm concerned, unless something else is uncovered there is nothing else to do. The cause of death has been determined and it is unclear whether or not the girl was pushed or fell against the timber spike and died. Hopefully, what we've uncovered will be enough to help the police solve the case. I assume there is other evidence for them to review. Oh, once we get the laboratory report on the degree of Relaxin in her system, that information might help us determine how long she was pregnant prior to her miscarriage. I also forgot to mention that DNA can be extracted from human embryo tissue, but currently there is no molecular biology test for the embryonic membrane tissue we found." Dr. Peterson said.

"I wonder if the girl shared a single outhouse facility with her siblings and parents, since this particular group of Amish are quite strict? Is it possible to retrieve a DNA sample from waste buckets?" Smith asked.

"I'd say it is, but not very likely in this case. You are welcome to go get the bucket from their outhouse and we can take a look. However, with a large family I'd imagine their waste bucket has been emptied several times since her miscarriage," Dr. Peterson replied.

"If they don't have running water, Amish use their waste for fertilizer. But during the winter I think they burn it. It's probably too late to pursue trying to obtain DNA from a piece of embryo in a waste bucket. No doubt it's been destroyed already," Smith commented. *In 1988, I wonder if the Amish still use outhouses or do, they have flushing toilets?*

What a relief! I'm not really excited about digging around in somebody else's poop and soiled toilet paper looking for a small embryo, Dr. Peterson thought. "Well, if that's it for today, I have a few more things to do before I meet my mom for dinner. We're meeting at a restaurant that specializes in fried fish. I think it's called Stroh's Annex. I've never been there before, but mother says the fish are to die for. I shouldn't eat fried food, but occasionally I do."

"I know what you mean. My physician tells me the same thing, but I like the taste of fried food even if it kills me."

"It's your body Paul. Do what you want. Even though I too would usually advise against eating anything fried."

"Okay doctor," Smith said. "Maybe I should take my physician's recommendations more seriously."

"Yes, maybe so."

Smith looked at his watch, it was almost 5:00 p.m. "Good job, doctor," Smith said. "Let's go get cleaned up." With that pronouncement, Peterson and Smith walked into the autopsy washroom, got rid of their gowns and the rest of their blood covered gear. They washed their hands, arms, and faces before departing the morgue to assume their other daily tasks. Smith said his goodbyes and again thanked Dr. Peterson for his help. He got into his car and departed the hospital. But before he left, he instructed Yoder to call Franklin Blair and tell him it was okay to retrieve Rachael's body. He also told Yoder to call the Sheriff's Department and tell Captain Moore that an autopsy report was being prepared and would be faxed to him the following morning.

Around 9:30 p.m., Dr. Peterson returned to the hospital after dining out with his mother. He needed to prepare a death certificate and write an autopsy report for the Coroner. He was pleased the Relaxin report was waiting for him on his desk upon his return. The report indicated a high level of Relaxin in the girl's system. Coupled with the fragment of the embryonic membrane found attached to the uterus and the increased amount of hormone in her system, there was no doubt that she had been pregnant. Dr. Peterson believed she was early into her first trimester of the pregnancy. And, due to the fact that there was no presence of an acute infection inside her uterus, Peterson reasoned the miscarriage occurred several days prior to her death. He also concluded that there was no way to scientifically determine if the deceased was pushed into or fell back on the spike. However, the bruising on the girl's shoulders suggested the possibility that she may have been pushed. An hour later he finished the autopsy report and the death certificate. He left the documents on top of Smith's desk inside the morgue for him to read, approve, and sign the following morning.

Chapter 5

Jacob and Sarah Miller left their house at 8:30 a.m. on Wednesday to pick up Rachael's coffin. Amos Miller, Jacob's second cousin, who was a cabinet and coffin maker, promised to have Rachael's wooden coffin completed by 10:00 a.m. The couple left their home to pick-up the coffin and drop off Rachael's clothing and the coffin to Blair-Samuel's Funeral Home in Wayne. Sarah picked out a freshly pressed and cleaned, Sunday dress, cap, apron, socks, and undergarments for the morticians to adorn Rachael's corpse with in her coffin. Jacob brought along some rope to secure the coffin onto the back of their large family buggy. It was a twenty-minute ride to his cousin's adjacent residence and shop.

Horse and buggies can travel 8-10 miles an hour in good weather. But in winter time with cold weather, slick and ice-covered roads, the speeds are lower. Amos' shop was located two miles to the south of County Road W200S and two miles east from there. Wayne was less than eight miles from Amos' home.

Amos Miller was ten years older than his cousin, Jacob. Amos was forty-eight years old and his mother and Jacob's mother were sisters. As expected, Amos made the coffin perfectly sized to fit Rachael at the cost of the lumber, as agreed between the cousins. He charged nothing for his labor. Amos was shocked to learn of Rachael's death, as was the rest of the extended Miller family. He wondered if an "English" criminal might have accosted and killed the fifteen-year-old girl. *It would not be a shock*, he thought.

Upon arriving at Amos' shop, Jacob tied the buggy horse to a post, covered it with a blanket, and gave it water, and a couple of carrots to eat. He and Sarah entered the shop. They immediately saw a plain white pine coffin atop a work bench. The inside and outside of the coffin were unfinished and there was no fancy lace padding lining the inside of the casket. The Millers assumed the small coffin was for Rachael.

When Sarah saw the coffin, she had to grasp the top of the work bench to steady herself. Reality was finally setting in. In the not too distant future, she would see the remains of her fourth-born child Rachael lying inside the casket. Sarah gasped for air, felt light-headed, and then began to sob. She appeared to be losing consciousness as she stared at the casket. Jacob sensed she was in trouble and he clung to her. He held her up and assured her that things would be all right. "God will take care of everything," he said, speaking softly to her. A few minutes later, Sarah seemed to improve. The color in her face was returning to normal. Jacob remembered telling her that it would be a hard day. Nevertheless, she insisted on accompanying him to Amos' shop and the funeral home.

A minute later, Amos walked into the shop and greeted

Jacob and Sarah. "I made a sturdy coffin for Rachael. May God bless her soul and keep her safe in his forgiving arms forever."

"Amen," Jacob replied. "Thank you, Amos for helping us during our time of need. The viewing will begin tomorrow morning at 10:00 a.m. in our house."

"We plan to be there. Marietta already told me she'd bring some food to share after the burial service."

"Thank you, that would be appreciated," Sarah said, perking up a little bit.

"I'll have her make a raisin-filled funeral pie," Amos said with a sympathetic smile.

"Thank you so much," Sarah responded, while wiping a tear from the corner of her eye.

"Is there anything else we can do for you?" Amos asked.

"I think you have done enough for us already, cousin. We appreciate it. Thank you," Jacob replied.

Amos helped his cousin load the empty coffin onto the back of the buggy. They secured it with rope and several minutes later they were inside the buggy headed toward Wayne. The ride took longer than they anticipated, but they finally arrived around noon at the Blair-Samuels mortuary. Jacob met with Franklin Blair, who directed them to bring the coffin to the rear of the funeral home, where they unloaded it. Sarah handed Rachael's funeral garments to Blair.

Blair thanked her and assured her again they would

take care of everything, hopefully to the family's satisfaction. "We will be picking-up Rachael's body in about an hour. We'll take great care to make sure she is properly dressed, secured in the coffin, and ready for the funeral services," Blair assured them.

"When will you return Rachael to our home?" Miller inquired.

"It will be early Thursday around 8:00 a.m. if everything goes as planned," Blair stated plainly.

"Thank you for your help, Mr. Blair. I'll pay you tomorrow."

"You can pay me at your convenience," Blair stated.

"No, thanks. I always pay my bills on-time and in cash," Miller said firmly.

"That will be fine. Thank you both once again for allowing me to serve your family at this most difficult time," Blair said sincerely.

When Jacob and Sarah returned home, they assembled their family in the living room and talked to them about Rachael's viewing, funeral, and burial ceremonies. Jacob reminded his children of the importance of the Amish values of simplicity, humility, and mutual aid. He said, "When our church members, family, and friends offer condolences, remember that there will be no praise given for Rachael. Only God and the church community will receive the praise and any tribute for her life on earth." Jacob cautioned his children to take a reserved approach to grief. He instructed them not to show their emotions too much during the public ceremonies. Jacob emphasized that their personal grieving must be done in private. And, he repeated the message of the Amish faith that, when you die you will immediately be with God. Speaking directly to his children, he asked, “Do any of you have any questions?”

Jonathan got up from the couch and said, “When will Rachael be returned to us?”

“The undertaker said we’ll have Rachael back sometime early tomorrow morning. So, that doesn’t give us much time to prepare.”

“Have you decided who will dig her grave?” Jonathan asked.

“That decision will be made by the men in our church community. They will dig the grave and take care of our daily chores which includes feeding the livestock and chickens. They will do whatever is needed to maintain the farm. The decedent’s family is never expected to do those things,” Miller said. “In addition, the church ladies will be busy cleaning the house and clearing the office area where Rachael’s coffin will be placed for viewing and the funeral service, later this afternoon.”

When Jacob was finished instructing his family, they helped him remove the heavier items of furniture in the open office, where Rachael’s body would lie in state, alone and atop a large oak desk. All the furniture in the big living room was moved to the barn and a hundred or so folding chairs were lined up in rows inside the space.

After a quick supper, the family departed for bed. It was doubtful any of them would get much rest. Sarah tried her best to sleep, but the thought of her deceased daughter lying in their home the following day, made it impossible for her to rest. She tossed and turned most of the night and awoke the following morning exhausted. Jacob managed to rest for a few hours, then lay awake watching over his restless wife for the rest of the night.

* * *

On Thursday morning at 6:00 a.m. the family awoke. Everyone got up early to clean up, dress conservatively in black, and straighten up the house in preparation for the anticipated crowd of church members and family coming to offer their condolences. Normally, the viewing would go on for two days, but because of the autopsy and embalming, the viewing would only occur on Thursday. Her funeral service would take place on Friday morning from 10:00 a.m. until noon. The burial would follow on Friday afternoon and would be open to every member of the church community. Extended family members and close friends would be welcome to join the immediate family for a meal following the burial.

The funeral home's white van arrived with Rachael's remains inside the casket precisely at 8:00 a.m. The coffin was secured inside the interior of the van with strong nylon straps. Blair and his associate helped Jacob and Jonathan unstrap the coffin and carry it inside the home. The coffin was placed atop a desk in a separate room. When the top of the coffin was removed, Rachael's body was revealed inside the plain wooden casket. Jacob and Sarah were the first to view their eldest daughter inside the wooden tomb. There were no cosmetics or enhancements applied to her face. She was as she appeared in the barn two days before, pale and lifeless. Her eyes were closed as if she were in a deep sleep. Her flesh was covered in plain garments.

Sarah looked at her daughter inside the coffin and almost collapsed again. The reality of the event appeared to overwhelm her. She broke out in tears and the rest of the family surrounded her. Jacob quickly grabbed her before she fell and lowered her onto one of the folding chairs in the living room. The family tried to offer comfort, but the death of a child to a parent usually is unbearable, horrible, and unimaginable. There can never be enough care or comforting to make any parent feel comfortable or balanced at those times.

The disturbing vision of her deceased child lying in the casket would remain etched in Sarah's psyche for the rest of her life. Nora, Sarah's thirteen-year-old daughter, made a cup of meadow tea for her mother. The warm mint-flavored liquid seemed to calm her slightly and she slowly regained her composure. Her nine-year-old, Lydia, placed a foot rest under her feet. Sarah smiled at her children, who surrounded her and were trying to comfort her as best they could.

The church's Bishop, Harold Mishler, and one of the church ministers, Samuel Zook, arrived at the Miller residence at 9:45 a.m. They paid their respects and offered their condolences to the family. Mishler and Zook would officiate at the funeral service held in the Miller home the following day.

The two-hour funeral service to be held on Friday would be spoken in German, as would be the religious sermons and songs. Usually, the Amish sing familiar songs at funerals, out of the Ausbund, the Amish church hymnal.

The Miller's received an unexpected and unusual "English" visitor to their daughter's viewing around 3:00 p.m. Detective Moore, drove to their home, parked his police cruiser along the road, and walked toward their residence. He was amazed when he saw the number of Amish buggies parked everywhere in the yard, on the road, and in the dirt road adjacent to the barn. He imagined, there were at least one-hundred fifty Amish in attendance at the viewing. He never anticipated seeing that many people. Moore was in plain clothes and wore an overcoat and a hat. When Jacob saw him standing inside his kitchen, he was surprised. Moore was one of the few "English" he'd ever seen at an Amish viewing. He appreciated his presence, but wondered why the police detective was there. It was a subtle reminder that the local authorities were going to be involved in the case until someone was caught and held accountable for Rachael's death.

When he saw Jacob and Sarah dressed in their Sunday best in the living room and away from the coffin, Moore was curious as to why the mood in the room appeared to be so solemn. There was no speaking. The attendees sat quietly in the chairs and appeared to be praying. Normally, during a viewing in the Presbyterian funeral services he'd attended, the family and visitors seemed noisier and more upbeat. As he waited in line to talk to the Millers, he quietly asked an older Amish man about their religious customs. He was not surprised to learn that, in the Amish tradition when someone dies, it signals the end of their worldly life and begins their life in the hereafter with God. Moore also learned it was their unique custom to offer condolences to the surviving loved ones, but not to mention anything about the character of the deceased person or to praise the decedent. He learned that God and the Amish church community are to be praised, but not the deceased.

About ten minutes after he got into the line to view Rachael's remains, he arrived at the coffin. The casket sat in a small room by itself away from the living room. Mr. and Mrs. Miller and their children stood in the large living room and watched as the church community separately progressed by the coffin. There was no talking in the line to see the body, except the conversation Moore had with the one attendee. Moore concluded viewings at Amish funerals are very solemn events and totally different than what he'd been used too. Nevertheless, he smiled and said to the Millers, "I just wanted to come by and offer my condolences to both of you. You and your family are in my prayers."

"Thank you, Detective Moore," Miller responded appreciatively. "We did not expect to see you for the next several days. But we thank you coming to see us."

"Well, as you know, I planned to question you again concerning the facts surrounding Rachael's demise. However, I knew you were going to be busy for the next several days. I'll contact you this coming Monday, if that's alright with you?"

"Yes, that sounds fine. Thank you for coming to pay

your respects," the Amish man replied solemnly.

Detective Moore thought he observed more than surprise in the Amish man's face after Miller saw him standing in his home. For a brief moment, Moore thought he detected remorse in the man's facial expression and eyes. He wondered, *why did Miller look remorseful? Was Miller involved somehow in her demise?* Moore hoped not, but he'd seen plenty of awful things in his time as a police detective. For now, Moore considered every person in the Miller household a potential suspect, with the exception of the younger children.

* * *

The funeral was held inside the Millers' home on Friday morning. Many people were crammed into the small chairs in the living room. The funeral service lasted two hours. Bishop Mishler and Zook, one of the church ministers, conducted a grave-side burial service at 1:00 p.m. following the funeral service. It was understood that all church members could attend. The burial was conducted in their usual language of Pennsylvania Dutch. The service ended after the final prayer was spoken, the coffin lowered into the grave, and completely covered with dirt. Generally, graves are marked by wooden plaques. The name, birth date, and death date are sometimes etched into the wood, which was done on Rachael's marker to denote the location of her grave. Sometimes, children's markers lie flat on the ground and can be marked or unmarked depending on the custom of the individual church community. Rachael's marker stood upright. The grave marker was made of hard wood. It was expected the marker would decay and wear away over time. The use of unnamed wooden markers deemphasizes the importance of the individual, which is a cornerstone of the Amish tradition. But named markers, like Rachael's, were also acceptable.

The Miller family, extended family, and close friends returned to their home for a funeral meal following the burial. A typical Amish funeral meal is chicken and noodles, bologna sandwiches, potato salad, cake, pies, jello with fruit, and plenty of coffee. The Miller's funeral meal was no exception.

After their guests departed, Jacob reminded his family that for the next year they would wear black clothes to indicate they were in mourning for the loss of Rachael. He also told them Amish etiquette was to expect frequent visits from family and friends during that same time period.

Chapter 6

Captain Moore and Sergeant Chilcott arrived at the Miller residence early Monday afternoon. Moore's plan was to interview Jacob and Sarah Miller, Rachael's parents, and Jonathan Miller, Joshua Miller, James Miller, and Nora Miller, her siblings. All were adults or in their teens. They were all being looked at as possible suspects, except the women, in the Rachael Miller homicide case.

Initially, Sergeant Chilcott indicated he suspected a member or members of the Miller family to have been the perpetrator of the crime. Moore tried to deter him from forming a preliminary opinion without knowing all the facts of the case. He advised him to keep an open mind.

Chilcott was aware of incidents of crime in the Amish community, but he never dealt with them directly before. But, some of the other officers on the force had worked on criminal cases involving the Amish. Usually, the Amish covered those things up and dealt with them in their church communities. It was almost an unwritten rule that the Amish would not be prosecuted for certain crimes, even as bad as incest, unless violence was involved. The Amish do not believe in the concept of prosecution and incarceration for the sins they commit. Instead, they prefer to deal with sin within the church community.

Detective Moore was advised by Jacob Miller that he would speak for the family. This presented an immediate problem for Moore. The Prosecutor and Sheriff would expect Moore to interview the Millers individually, as is the practice in most investigatory proceedings. So, Moore pondered, *how am I to do it without Jacob Miller's permission?* He decided it might be necessary to compromise to some degree in order to conduct the interviews.

After all, no one can be compelled to give a statement, even if they are detained or arrested. If Moore detained any of the Millers, those individuals would not need to be Mirandized, unless they were questioned. Generally, the police would rather speak to witnesses without having to arrest them and give them the Miranda warning. Legally, statements from minors can be obtained with or without a court order. Moore knew children under 14 would need to have a parent or guardian present during their interrogation. Children 14 years-of-age or older would not require a representative present while being interrogated. But the law allows a parent to refuse police to interrogate any minor child. However, it would look very fishy if the father of a deceased girl tried to impede the investigation of his daughter's probable homicide.

Moore hoped to convince Miller to allow most of the individual members of his family to be interviewed alone. If not, Moore thought his fallback proposition would be to ask Jacob Miller if he would allow his children to be interviewed as long as Miller was present with them.

Detective Moore had already spent the weekend going over specific questions he would ask each of the Millers if given the chance. He wanted to start with Mrs. Miller, because she seemed to be the most emotionally distraught. It was totally understandable; Rachael was Sarah's first-born girl and that is a significant event for many women.

The normal procedure when conducting a formal interview involves using a video camera. Chilcott reminded him that the Amish do not allow specific photographs of themselves, unless it is absolutely a government requirement. "Photographs are not against an Amish person's religion," Chilcott told him, "but the Amish do prohibit posing for photographs." Posing may be seen as a show of pride. Many Amish completely refuse to allow themselves to be photographed. Chilcott proposed to Moore that they should use an old-fashioned voice recording device in lieu of a video camera. Moore agreed.

Moore and Chilcott arrived on the Miller's doorstep at 1:15 p.m. Chilcott carried a briefcase with the small battery-operated recording device inside. Moore carried an regular sized, lined yellow tablet. He also possessed the Rachael Miller case file, which he held behind the tablet. Moore knocked on the door and waited. Within a minute, Sarah Miller appeared and invited them to come inside. She offered them a cup of coffee, tea, or water and also invited them to sit down at the kitchen table. Moore placed the case file along with the lined tablet in front of him on the table. After several minutes, Jacob Miller appeared in the room. He welcomed them to his home, but reminded

Moore about his ground rule that he'd previously established concerning interviewing his family.

Moore acknowledged the Millers' greeting and wished them a belated Merry Christmas. He commented, "It probably was a difficult Christmas for you, but praise to God for welcoming Rachael into heaven."

Miller responded, "This Christmas will always be remembered and especially cherished. Jesus' birth fulfilled God's promise to Rachael and every believer in him. And, that assurance was she'd receive forgiveness for her sins and be redeemed. We're confident that she's with God at this very moment.

"It's the blessing of Christmas that has been promised throughout the ages," Moore replied.

"Yes, it is and we are very thankful," Miller said sincerely.

"You have been blessed," Moore agreed. After several seconds of quiet reflection, Detective Moore began, "Mr. Miller, I have been assigned by the Grant County Prosecutor's office to determine what happened to your daughter. I need you to allow me to proceed slightly differently than you have suggested. I know you are trying to protect your family, but it is my job to help you do that as well. I have no intention of putting any of your family members in jeopardy. My job is simply to find out what happened to Rachael and proceed accordingly. I cannot force any of you to give us a statement, but by putting conditions on my standard police investigative procedures that makes me wonder why you would do that."

"I am more than willing to give as many statements as you want, but the Amish tradition dictates that the husband should always speak for the family. And, that is what I am supposed to do. I want you to find out who did this horrible thing to my daughter and I will help you in any way I can."

"May I call you Jacob, Mr. Miller?

"Yes, that's fine."

"Jacob, I need all the help I can get to solve this crime, because, as the facts are unfolding thus far, it is apparent to me that this case is going to be very difficult to solve and bring to a successful conclusion. I need you to allow me to do my level best to help you," Moore said unapologetically.

"I'm hopeful you will provide us with answers," Miller said plainly.

"Well then, let me do my job as I have been trained to do it, sir. How about we do this. Let me take the statements from your family members without any input from you. You can still be in the room to observe. Would that work for you?"

Miller hesitated a moment and then looked at his wife. She leaned over and said something in his ear. He thought for a brief moment and then responded to Moore, "Alright, that will work."

"One more thing," Moore added, "I'll need you to keep everyone out of the kitchen area while the interviews are underway, except for yourself and the person being interviewed. Is that agreeable to you?"

"Yes, that's fine." Miller said, pointing to his wife and instructing her to handle the children.

Chilcott said nothing to Moore, but he gave him a favorable look as if to say, *I'm surprised you were able to persuade this stubborn and not well-educated Amish man to do the right thing.* So far, Detective Moore was impressing Chilcott with the persuasive abilities he possessed. For the moment, Chilcott knew Moore only wanted him to observe. Captain Moore was grooming him to be a full-fledged detective and he was ready to learn.

Miller sat down at the kitchen table and said to Moore, "I'll be happy to give my statement first.

"That's fine." Moore said as he turned to Chilcott and said, "Sergeant Chilcott, will you please set up the tape recorder prior to our taking Jacob's statement."

Chilcott retrieved the small recording device from his briefcase and placed a cassette tape into the recorder. He plugged a small cable into the back of the machine and connected it to a microphone. Chilcott placed the microphone into a stand and placed it on the kitchen table between Miller and Moore. He checked the device and said to Moore, "You can begin."

Talking directly into the microphone, Moore stated, "This is Captain Clarence J. Moore of the Grant County Sheriff's Department. I'm at the home of Jacob Miller on W200S in Grant County, Ohio. Today's date is December 26, 1988 and it's 1:33 p.m. I am taking a statement from Mr. Jacob Miller in regards to the death of his daughter, Rachael.

Moore's first question to Miller was, "What was your relationship to the deceased?"

"I'm the girl's father," Miller stated.

"Mr. Miller did you love your daughter?"

Miller gave the detective a funny look, nodded, and said, "Yes."

"What was Rachael's birth date?"

"November 5, 1973."

"So, that means she just turned fifteen, correct?"

"Yes."

"Was Rachael well-liked by others in the church, at school, and in this area of the county?"

"Yes, she had many friends."

"Did Rachael have any enemies that you are aware of?"

"No."

"Did she get along well with you, Mrs. Miller, and her siblings?

"Yes."

"Do you know of any time someone tried to hurt her or make her feel bad?"

"No, other than when she was a little girl. We spanked her in order to discipline her. The Amish church views spanking as acceptable. Spanking is used to break a child's will, but it must be done with the right motives and state of mind."

"Understood. My parents spanked me as well," Moore replied with a smile. "I usually got from them what I deserved."

"Amish view spanking as their method of dealing with their children's rebellious nature and disobedience," Miller explained. "But we never hit Rachael."

Moore didn't quite understand the distinction, but he proceeded with his questioning. "Did she have a boyfriend or someone special outside the family in her life?"

"She had lots of friends, boys and girls, as I previously told you."

"Was there someone special?"

"Several boys seemed interested in being with her."

"Can you give me their names, please?"

"I can't, but my wife probably could help you with that."

"Have you noticed there was anything stolen or missing in the barn following the incident?"

"No. Nothing of value was stored in the barn other than the animals and a few saddles, harnesses, and such."

"Were you aware that Rachael has been sexually active?" Moore asked abruptly, completely catching Miller off guard.

Miller looked directly at Moore, and then at his wife, who just entered the kitchen with a stack of towels, and then again quickly back at Moore. Miller had an astonished look in his eyes, redness in his round face, and in a sudden bolt of anger he spoke, "Please lower your voice Detective and remember that there are young children in this house. No, I was not aware, but how do you know about her activities?" Miller fired back.

"I'm very sorry. That is why it might be better to continue these interviews in my office in Wayne, Mr. Miller. Rachael's autopsy revealed she had been pregnant and that she had a miscarriage several days prior to her death."

"That can't be possible, there must be some mistake," Miller blurted out angrily.

"I have the autopsy report here in the case file. Should I read the findings for you?"

"Yes, please do," the distraught Amish man insisted.

"I think it best if you read the part about her sexual activity and miscarriage for yourself," Moore stated. He handed the report to Miller and pointed to where the information about the pregnancy began.

Moore watched as Mr. and Mrs. Miller read that portion of the report. He observed that they were both upset and looked sad as they read about their young daughter, Rachael.

"What happened to the baby?" Mrs. Miller asked.

"I have no idea, but my assumption is the embryo was probably shed from her body on the toilet. Undoubtedly, there was a lot of bleeding. Probably very similar to when she would have a period."

"I have no idea what to think or say," Miller said sadly.

His head drooped as he spoke, "It is very disheartening to think Rachael had sex out of wedlock, became pregnant, and miscarried a baby."

"With that information in mind, who do you think the baby's father might have been?"

"I have no idea," Miller replied shaking his head.

Referring to his notes, Moore asked Mr. Miller, "Did she have any regular male visitors during the last several months?"

"No, I don't think so."

"Please forgive me, but I need to ask this question. Mr. Miller, did you ever have sexual relations with Rachael?'

Miller's faced turned beet red and he looked at Moore with disgust and anger and said, "No, what kind of man and father do you think I am?"

"Did you kill Rachael or have anything to do with her death?"

"Absolutely not!"

"I'm extremely sorry I have to ask these questions, but please understand this is my job. I believe you are a good and loving father," Moore stated sincerely. Previously, Moore wondered if the elder Miller was involved. But there were no telltale signs of lying exhibited by Miller. His answers were direct and quick. He showed no signs of trying to make excuses or lie. After questioning Miller and seeing his reactions, Moore believed he was not involved in Rachael's demise. And, his instincts and questioning confirmed he'd made the right decision to not Mirandize

Jacob Miller.

"Thank you, Detective," Miller said as he appeared to be regaining his composure.

"I understand. If I were in your shoes my questions would have upset me as well."

"Let's go on then," Miller stated.

"Do you have any idea why Rachael was in the barn that evening? You told me your family normally goes to bed around 9:00 p.m., which is about the time of her death."

"No, I do not. As you might recall, I told you I had fallen asleep in my recliner reading the Bible. I was not paying any attention to Rachael's activities after supper."

"Did Rachael frequently go outdoors at night?"

"Well, yes, sometimes she did. We all enjoy breathing in fresh air, taking a walk, and viewing God's creation. But I never considered it necessary to ask the older kids where they were going. We keep better track of the younger ones, and check on them more frequently."

"Did she go to the barn frequently at night?"

"Occasionally, she would go to the barn to check on her pony. She loved the little Shetland I originally bought for all the kids ten years ago. But the horse kind of took to her. She named the horse Dusty, I guess due to its color, which is rusty brown. She liked to talk to the horse and comb its long, coarse mane."

"Outside the family, do you employ anyone to help

around the farm?"

"No, with eleven children it is not necessary," Miller replied with a smile.

"Do you ever have any frequent visitors who come to see you at the farm?"

"Only Amos, my cousin, who comes for lunch with his wife, Marietta, every now and again."

"Do you have any reason to suspect Amos might have harmed or wanted to harm Rachael?" Moore asked.

"I would trust Amos with my life and my family's lives. He's been a wonderful friend and he and my other relatives helped me build this house, barn, and utility building. We all attend the same church and live under the strict Amish traditions as depicted in the Ordnung," Miller explained.

"What is the Ordnung?" Moore asked having never heard the term used.

"It is a document that lays out rules and guidelines for our daily living and it is agreed to and abided by the members of our church community. All Old Order Amish agree to an Ordnung, but in each church community there are some differences."

"I don't have any more questions for you at this time, but if you think of something that might be important, please contact me. Thank you for your cooperation. I'm sorry I had to ask you some very difficult questions and to have informed you about some unpleasant and personal things about Rachael. I am only doing my job as I have been taught."

"Thank you, Detective. I can see that it has been difficult for you as well. Our prayers are that you will quickly find the person responsible for her death. Would you like to take a break and have some coffee or tea before you get started interviewing my wife?"

"Yes, but I need to visit your facilities too." He said smiling. Moore got up from the table and Miller pointed him to the bathroom next to the kitchen.

Chapter 7

When Moore returned from his visit to the bathroom, he briefly stood next to the Millers' stove to warm himself. Miller and his wife, Sarah, watched patiently trying to imagine Moore's next move. He thought, *I'd never realized Amish have gas motors outside that pump water into the house to allow for indoor toilets similar to mine.* He remembered Chilcott's comment that many Old Order Amish bathe on Wednesday and Saturday nights. Saturday's baths or showers are done in preparation for their Sunday worship services. *I guess if they only want two baths a week, so be it.* "It's cold outside," Moore stated as he stood by the hot stove making a casual comment.

"Yes, it's really cold and it's supposed to be getting colder as the day progresses. I think we have four inches of accumulated snow already. I'm going to have to carry in more firewood for the stove before we run out," Miller declared.

"I think you folks might get more snow in northern Ohio than I'm used to," Moore said trying to establish a friendly and relaxed mood. "My wife and I moved here from downtown Chicago a few months ago. We get snow in Chicago, but not as much as I've been told you get here in Grant County."

"Yes, we get lots of it during the wintertime," Miller commented.

Moore sat down at the table, took a sip of tepid tea, checked his notes, and asked Sarah Miller if she was ready to be interviewed.

Mrs. Miller replied, "Yes."

Moore waited for Chilcott to turn on the recorder and push the microphone between the two of them.

Sarah Miller was thirty-eight years old. She was short, slightly plump, and seemed perfectly content with her Amish lifestyle. Moore estimated her height at five-feet even. She had brown eyes and brown hair. Her hair was parted in the middle of her head, gathered around into a knot, and was tucked just under the edges of her white Amish covering, also referred to as a prayer cap. Most women in the Amish community wore them and black bonnets. Young girls are allowed to wear black bonnets only on Sunday mornings to church. The older girls and women can wear a plain white covering or a black bonnet. Sarah wore a plain black homemade dress with hooks and eyes and a white apron. The Millers married when she was eighteen years-old. Jonathan was born about ten months after their wedding ceremony.

Moore smiled at Sarah as he began to formulate his first question. "Would you like me to call you Mrs. Miller or would Sarah be alright?"

"You can call me Sarah, if you like, Detective."

"Good, let's begin, Sarah. How close would you say you were to Rachael?"

"Very close."

"Did she tell you that she was sexually active and had become pregnant?"

"No; I had no idea."

"Why do you suppose she hid the truth from you?"

"I don't think children in general tell their parents everything they experience in life, particularly if it's of a shameful nature. I know through studying the Bible that I am not perfect and neither is anyone else," Sarah replied with a solemn look on her face. "But that is why acknowledgement of our sins and being forgiven for them is so important, particularly, if we someday intend to be with God."

"Yes, I totally agree with you," Moore replied. "Did you love Rachael?"

"Of course, I did. I'd say most mothers would say they loved their children, no matter what life choices their children might make."

"Your husband told me Rachael was well-liked and had lots of friends. Would you agree?"

"Yes, she was a very nice person, Detective. It's too bad you'll never get to know her."

"Agreed," Moore said smiling. "Did Rachael have any enemies that you were aware of?"

"No, Detective."

"Was there anyone in your immediate family, who Rachael did not get along with?"

"No; not that I'm aware of."

"Did anyone make her feel bad or want to hurt her?" Moore asked.

"No; not that I'm aware of."

"Alright. Did Rachael ever mention she had a boyfriend or someone special in her life?"

"Yes, there were two young Amish men, who expressed an interest in going out with her six months ago."

"How do you know that?"

"Because she told me."

"Alright. Did she tell you who they were?"

"No, but I understood them to be a few years older than she was and that they had been in school with her. You could ask her former teacher. She might be able to identify them for you."

"That's a good idea," Moore said. He handed her a small notepad out of his inside coat pocket along with a pen and then said, "Sarah, would you please write down the teacher's name, the school's name, and the location of the school."

Sarah quickly provided the information Moore requested and handed the notepad and pen back to him.

"Thank you, Sarah," Moore said sincerely. "Following the incident, did you notice anything of value missing from either the barn or inside your home?"

"No."

"Okay. Do you have any recollection of what you were doing the night of the homicide between 7:00 p.m. and 9:00 p.m., just prior to going to your bedroom?"

"Yes, I was knitting in the living room."

"What was Jacob doing between those hours?"

"He was reading the Bible, but then he fell asleep," Sarah said with a grin.

"I take your grin to mean that it is usual for him to fall asleep in the evening in his chair."

"Yes; normally I wake him up when I go to bed. But because he seemed extra tired, I let him sleep. He came to bed around 9:30 p.m."

"How do you know what time he came to bed?"

"I'm a very light sleeper. With eleven children to be concerned about, I think most wives would tell you the same thing. I remember looking at my alarm clock when I felt the mattress move indicating he was in bed."

"How many Amish boys have come to visit Rachael at home during the last year?"

"Not hesitating at all, Sarah said, "None."

"If Rachael didn't have any visitors, how do you explain her pregnancy? Obviously, someone was responsible for impregnating her."

"I really have no idea."

"Is it possible that it might have been someone in this

household?"

"No! All my boys were raised right. None of them would have done such a terrible thing to their sister," Sarah declared crossly.

"Unfortunately, I'm not so sure based on the evidence I've seen thus far," Moore said unapologetically. "For the moment let's proceed, shall we?"

"I assume you have heard rumors about that sort of behavior in the Amish community, but it does not apply to my family, Detective."

"Assuming you are correct, then there must have been someone else that she was sexually active with. Wouldn't you agree?"

"Yes, it would seem so," Sarah admitted regrettably.

"So, maybe that person was in the barn with her that evening. And, maybe they decided to have relations, but at the last minute she changed her mind. Could that person have been her father?"

"No, Jacob would never do such a thing! I am a good and accommodating woman. He would have no reason to seek another for attention."

"It would seem so, but you never know what people might do under the right circumstances."

"Well, we've been married twenty years and I think I know him better than you do. That sort of thing would never enter his mind," Sarah said firmly.

"Let's move on then. Alright, if Jacob didn't do it and

your boys didn't do it. Then, who impregnated Rachael?"

"I don't know, Detective. That is your job to determine who the guilty party is. Maybe it's a secret lover, one of those older boys from school, who expressed an interest in going out with her. Maybe it was an unknown assailant."

"Yes, those are valid possibilities and I will pursue every lead. However, answering the question of who was sexually active with Rachael does not necessarily solve the crime. It only provides us with one piece of information to this puzzle. The baby's father and the killer may not be the same person. In fact, I've even thought her death might have been accidental. She could have been in the barn innocently petting and looking after Dusty, lost her balance somehow, and fell back on the spike."

"That sounds more probable to me rather than accusing one of her siblings to be her fornicator and perhaps her killer."

"Are you aware that consenting family members can engage in incest in Ohio, and not be prosecuted? Unless, that is, if it involves violence, rape, or a parental figure."

"Our family lives by God's rules and not by the rules governing Ohio. It is a terrible sin to engage in incest and to deliberately kill another."

Moore briefly paused and then said, "Do you have any idea why Rachael might have been in the barn that evening?"

"At this point, I have no idea. She could have gone out to the barn to think about the terrible ramifications of her illicit sexual activity. Or, she could have gone out to comb

Dusty's mane as my husband suggested. My hope is she was out there praying for forgiveness to almighty God for the sins she committed."

"Understood," Moore replied sympathetically. "I only have several more questions for you, Sarah, but this is a hard one. Do you have any knowledge of who killed Rachael?"

"Well, I certainly have no idea who might have taken her life, Detective. I could never do such a terrible thing."

"So, what you're saying is you are not covering up for one of your boys?"

"No, I'm not. They were all raised to be God-fearing, respectful, and loving children. They would never do such a thing to their own sister.

"Okay, thanks for your honest responses and tolerant attitude toward my questioning. I hope you realize I am just doing my job."

"Thank you, Detective. I appreciate your concern due to the necessary questioning, no matter how difficult or uncomfortable they were. I guess I understand those things needed to be asked under the circumstance. I'm just sorry we are involved in this situation. I hope you can get answers quickly, as to who took Rachael's life and who she was sexually active with. So, our good name can be cleared and this veil of accusations can be lifted."

"I'm doing my best, but as I initially told you this may take some time to unravel the true facts in this case. I don't have any more questions for you, but if you find out something that is important to this case, please contact me.” Moore looked at his watch. It was 4:00 p.m. He commented to Miller, “I think we’ll call it a day and resume questioning your four oldest children tomorrow starting at 9:00 a.m. Will that work for your schedule?” Moore asked.

“Yes, that would be fine. They will have most of their important chores done by then.”

“Okay Sergeant, let’s load up the equipment and head back to the office. We’ll see you in the morning folks,” Moore stated as he and Chilcott walked out the kitchen door.

Chapter 8

Detective Moore met Sergeant Chilcott for breakfast at the local diner Tuesday morning at 7:30 a.m. While waiting for breakfast to be served, Moore asked, "How do you think the questioning is progressing on the Miller case?"

"Pretty well, but I don't understand why you didn't Mirandize Jacob Miller? He's a potential suspect," Chilcott replied.

"No; that's where you're wrong, Sergeant. You saw him in the corner of the barn the morning after the homicide, didn't you? He was silent and solemnly grieving the loss of his daughter without displaying much passion."

"Yes, I did."

"He did not lose his composure, although I thought he might. It's something you'd expect to see from an Amish man. I've learned they do not show emotion in public. No matter what the circumstance. He was being consistent with his personal beliefs and that exhibits honest behavior."

"Well, maybe he was acting."

"I don't believe that for a minute. Did you hear the answers he gave during questioning? They were clear, concise, honest, and he did not ramble on trying to mislead me. His eyes were directed at me and he did not act nervous or seem confused. Liars usually shift in their seats, look away from the interrogator, and take long amounts of time to formulate their answers. Jacob Miller displayed none of that."

"Okay, you make some good points, Boss. But how about Mrs. Miller? I think she might have been lying to you?"

"I'm not sure she lied. But I wonder if she's telling me everything she knows. Mothers are certainly capable of trying to protect their children. She might suspect a family member, but she isn't going to volunteer that information straightforwardly. Do you remember what she said when asked about who might have gotten Rachael pregnant?"

"Not off the top of my head I don't. I'd need to refer to the tape recording."

"She said, 'No, all my boys were raised right.' She then went on to say the rumors about Amish people being involved in incest did not apply to her family. I don't recall bringing up incest until after she did. Plus, there were other things she said suggesting she didn't want to believe it could ever apply to her family. When push comes to shove, I think we can approach Mrs. Miller and talk about the value in confessing to a crime, rather than being implicated and convicted of a crime. In Ohio the statues allow incest as long as it doesn't involve a parental figure. However, this is a case of a possible homicide and possibly incest.

I've heard Ohio prosecutors don't normally prosecute for incest, unless it also involves rape or murder. And, as of yet, we don't have all the answers. But we know the law and she doesn't."

"So, what's your conclusion, Boss?"

"I think we need to pursue all the leads, as minor as they may be, until we can prove who impregnated Rachael. Once that's known, we can proceed to investigate who might have killed her. Was it the father of her baby or someone else? When we're finished with the interrogations, I think we need to contact the teacher at Rachael's school. What's her name and the name of the school?"

"I believe it's Hillcrest Amish School. The teacher's name is Linda Hershberger."

"Thank you. If we can finish interrogating the rest of family by the end of the day that would allow us to interview Ms. Hershberger on Wednesday."

"Sounds like a plan," Chilcott said with a grin.

Moore thought, *I hope we can get a break sooner rather than later.*

* * *

Chilcott's police cruiser pulled into the Miller driveway just before 9:00 a.m. They unbuckled their seat belts, collected their equipment and files, and proceeded to the home's rear entryway. Mr. and Mrs. Miller were in the kitchen waiting for them to arrive. After a brief greeting, Moore got down to business. "I'd like to talk to Jonathan first," Moore said emphatically.

A few minutes later Jonathan appeared in the kitchen and sat down at the kitchen table with the detectives and his father. Miller introduced Moore to his son. Mrs. Miller departed the room, claiming she needed to oversee the clothes washing.

"For the record Jonathan, how old are you?" Moore asked.

"Just turned nineteen years-old."

"As an adult, Jonathan, you don't have to have your father present in order for me to interview you."

Jonathan responded, "I'm alright with it, if he wants to stay."

Moore looked at Miller, who nodded his approval.

"Okay. I'm curious, why are you still living in this house with your parents? After all, most nineteen-year-old Amish men are already married and living on their own."

"Well, I have been saving money to get married and build a house. My parents are going to give me a few acres of their land in return for my help in running the farm."

"I take it you have a girlfriend that you plan to marry?"

"Yes, I do," Jonathan said proudly.

"Do you get along well with her?"

"Yes, I do."

"Are you sexually active with her?"

"Well, that's kind of personal isn't it, Detective. I'm a member of the church and I'm not supposed to be sexually active until we're married. But during Rumspringa we were," Jonathan revealed.

"I see. I've heard so much about Rumspringa, would you please tell me a little about it without going into great detail? Are the Amish kids free to have sex, drink lots of alcohol, do drugs, etc.? How long does that period last before you have to either join the church or leave?"

"Well, basically it lasts for two years. During this time, the sixteen-year-olds are allowed to live outside of the community without Amish restrictions. I chose to live at home and I did drink outside the house, but I never used drugs. Near the end of the two years was when my future wife and I got together. We had sex, but I always used protection. Some Amish kids go almost crazy with the antics they participate in. About twenty percent of them do not come back to the Amish life. I always knew I wanted to join the church community. Nevertheless, I did do some things contrary to the Amish rules. But now, I abide by the rules as specified in our local community Ordnung."

"Thank you for your honesty, Jonathan. It's really refreshing. What was your day like on Monday, December 19, 1988, you know, the day of your sister's death? What did you do that day?"

"I got up, brushed my teeth, washed my face, and went to the bathroom. Just the usual things. I fed the livestock at 4:30 a.m., cleaned some of the horse stalls, and groomed several horses. Then, I went back to the house, sat by the stove, and got warm. I ate an early lunch. After that, I read the Bible and checked on what my father wanted me to do for the rest of the day."

"Approximately how long did your chores take that morning?"

"I was pretty busy at least until 11:00 a.m."

"I assume you did other things that day."

"Yes, in the wintertime we usually clean and sharpen the implements, polish the horse saddles, make repairs around the farm, and sometimes take late afternoon naps."

"Did you take a nap that afternoon?"

"Yes, and when I awoke, Mom prepared dinner and we ate as a family at the kitchen table, as we always do."

"Okay. After dinner what did you do?"

"I'm building some wooden furniture in the workshop for my future home."

"How long did you do that?"

"About an hour and a half, I guess."

"When you left the workshop, did you see anything unusual outside the house? Did you see any lights on in the barn?"

"No, I didn't. I took a leak outside on my favorite bush and then came back inside our house. Seconds later, I walked up to my second-floor bedroom."

"Did anyone see you in the bedroom at that time?"

"Yes, my younger brother Peter was in the room. You see, I share a bedroom with my three younger brothers, Peter, James, and Joshua."

"How old is Peter?" Moore asked. "And, was he awake and did you talk to him?"

"Peter is eleven years-old. Yes, he was awake. We talked briefly until James and Joshua came to bed around 9:00 p.m."

"Okay. There's something about Rachael that I want to talk to you about," Moore said clearing his throat.

At that point Jacob Miller interrupted the questioning and said to Moore, "Do we really have to go there?"

"Unfortunately, Jacob, we do," Moore said plainly and then continued. "Jonathan, did you know Rachael was sexually active."

The Amish teen's face turned bright red and he said, "Are you sure about that. I doubt that very much. She wasn't even sixteen yet, and she was raised better than that!" Jonathan said angrily.

"I'm sorry, but it has been proven to be true."

Jonathan looked directly at his father and immediately saw sorrow register on his father's face.

Jacob nodded in acknowledgement of the fact that Rachael had been sexually active. Jacob Miller knew the next questions Moore was going to ask his son, as if he was clairvoyant.

"Jonathan, before you answer these questions, I would

like you to understand, you have the right to remain silent. Anything you say can and will be used against you in a court of law. You have the right to an attorney, and, if you cannot afford an attorney, one will be appointed for you. Do you understand me?"

"Yes, Detective Moore, I do."

"Good. Did you ever have sex with Rachael and did you have anything to do with her death?"

"No, to both of your questions, Detective."

Moore paused for a moment to give Jonathan an opportunity to reflect on the gravity of his answers, but then asked, "Are you absolutely sure?"

"I would never do either of those things to Rachael."

"Okay, let's proceed with my interrogation, shall we?"

"Ask away detective." Jonathan said. Moore noted his attitude and voice had changed from open and honest to annoyed and sarcastic.

Miller spoke up sharply to his son, "The man is only trying to do his job, Son. Be more respectful."

Jonathan nodded in acknowledgement of his father's authority and bowed his head.

"On the morning of Tuesday, December 20, 1988, you say you found your sister lying in the barn in a pool of blood."

"Yes, I did."

"When you discovered her body, what did you do? Did you touch her body?"

"I touched her face to see if she was still alive. She was not. Then, I sort of blacked out for a while, and then I ran to get my father after I regained my composure."

"Did you touch anything other than your sister's face, as you've stated?" Moore demanded.

"No. I told you, I went to the house to get my father. I led him to the spot where Rachael was lying on the barn floor. A half a minute or so later, my mother came to the spot followed by my siblings. We were all crying. After a few minutes, my father instructed me to harness one of the horses to our buggy, go to our closest "English" neighbor's home, use their telephone, and call the authorities for help."

"So, the buggy tracks in your driveway early Tuesday morning were from the trip you made to the neighbor's house to use the telephone?"

"Yes, that's correct."

"When you went into the barn on that Tuesday morning, did anything seem out of place or missing?"

"I don't think so, but I was more concerned about Rachael than anything else."

"Did you notice anyone near the barn at 4:30 a.m., when you went to feed the animals?"

"No."

"Since Rachael's death have you noticed anything missing in the barn or from the other out-buildings?"

"No; not that I can think of."

"Do you know anyone who might have wanted to hurt Rachael?"

"No."

"Thank you, Jonathan, for answering my questions. Some of the information you've given me might help solve this crime. I'm sorry I had to ask some very unsettling questions and reveal some delicate facts about Rachael to you. If you learn something else about this case, don't hesitate to contact me."

Moore looked at his wrist watch. The interview took almost an hour. He was sure they would be able to finish interviewing the rest of the oldest siblings before 4:00 p.m. The next person Moore wanted to interview was Joshua, another one of Rachael's brothers, who recently turned eighteen. Moore did the math and realized Miller and Sarah had been very busy giving birth to eleven children in their twenty-year marriage. He wondered whether at age thirty-eight Sarah, might want to slow the pace of having more babies to care for. Moore laughed under his breath and decided not to ask. He thought Jacob Miller was not lacking in the attention department. Moore also guessed Jonathan and his bride to be were not abstaining from having sex either, regardless of the rules of the church. Moore thought Jonathan was probably embarrassed discussing his sex life with his father who was present in the room.

Chapter 9

Following Jonathan Miller's interview, Moore checked his list of potential Miller family suspects and found Joshua next on his list. Prior to the interview, Moore took another bathroom break, got a fresh cup of hot tea, and told Miller that he wanted to interview Joshua next. Miller suggested to Moore that Mrs. Miller needed to be present, as well, to help with Joshua. Moore didn't understand the reason, but agreed to the request.

When Joshua was summed to the kitchen, he entered the room and it was clear to Moore that the boy had some mobility limitations and some other issues. He found the strange smile on Joshua's face to be unusual. He had an Amish-style bowl haircut. His hair was medium brown as were his eyes. He looked to be of medium height, but was overweight by at least thirty to forty-pounds. Moore thought at least half of the excessive pounds he weighed hung over his broadfall pants. Sarah Miller spoke after Joshua entered the room. "Let me talk to him before you proceed, alright?"

"Yes, that would be fine," Moore said realizing there was a problem with Joshua.

He watched as Mrs. Miller spoke slowly, clearly, and deliberately to the boy, who seemed to be more excited about the presence of a visitor in the house than anything else. “Just try to answer the man’s questions as best you can,” Mrs. Miller instructed her son. Moore noted Joshua seemed overly friendly and jovial. “Is Joshua all right?” Moore asked Mrs. Miller.

Sarah Miller immediately understood his question and realized Moore was unfamiliar with some of the common symptoms of a genetic disorder. “Joshua suffers with developmental and neurological disabilities, Detective. He was stricken with ‘Angelman syndrome’ as a young child. He is very lucky because he is now more high functioning, physically speaking. His condition has improved as an adult. Angelman syndrome can be treated, but there is no cure. I’ve been told somewhere in my family history there was a genetic flaw which, unfortunately he inherited from me. Technically, the doctors claim it was caused by a loss of function in a certain gene in the 15th chromosome. I’ve long forgotten the name of the gene, but the condition is very rare. It occurs in one in twelve to twenty-thousand people in the general population.”

“I’m so sorry,” Moore said sincerely. “Is he up for a few questions?” Moore asked politely. He realized that just because Joshua was lower functioning than the normal person didn’t mean he couldn’t recognize the truth.

“Yes, but he has a limited command of language and only uses a few words when he speaks. However, he has developed another means of communicating his message with expressions on his face and by nodding.”

"So, if I ask him a simple question, he will probably understand it and be able to communicate a response."

"Yes," Sarah said with a smile. "But please understand he is not retarded. He is low functioning intellectually speaking. Still, he can understand what is being presented to him as long as it is expressed in simple terms."

"I understand," Moore answered as he gazed across the table at Chilcott, who expressed a peculiarly troubling look on his face.

Chilcott wondered if Moore would give Joshua the Miranda warning, but he quickly decided Moore wouldn't. Obviously, it was going to be difficult to implicate Joshua for anything, even if it turned out he was guilty. It was clear, from the way Moore was handling this interview, he wasn't even sure Joshua was mentally able to stand trial. But he could provide some information as to how the other siblings treated Rachael and whether he saw anything suspicious the night of the possible homicide.

W*hat a case*, Moore thought. *Could it get any more complicated*? So, reluctantly, he proceeded with his questioning. "Good morning, Joshua." Moore began.

"Hello," Joshua said sweetly. There was a large smile on his face. Moore noted the size of his head seemed slightly smaller than it should have been and his teeth were unusually wide-spaced.

"My name is Clarence Moore and I'm a police officer. "If you want, you can call me Clarence, okay?"

"Hi … Clarence," Joshua said distinctly. His wide grin was still plastered on his face.

"I'm with the Grant County Sheriff's Department and I'm hoping to learn how Rachael died. Is it okay that I ask you some questions?"

"Yes," Joshua replied nodding his head up and down.

"Joshua, you are Rachael's older brother, right?"

"Yes."

"How old are you Joshua?"

"Eighteen."

"What kind of things do you do around the farm?"

"Feed chickens," Joshua said proudly.

"That's an important job."

"Yes," Joshua said nodding again.

"Did you and Rachael work together?"

"No."

"Why not?"

"She cooked and cleaned."

"I see." Moore paused briefly, then asked, "Did you love Rachael?"

"Yes."

"I guess she was very nice to you, right?"

"Yes."

"Would you ever harm anybody?"

"No," Joshua said smiling.

"Did you ever see anyone harm or hurt Rachael?"

"No."

"Do you know how Rachael got hurt?"

"No," he said shaking his head from right to left.

Moore asked cautiously, "Did you hurt Rachael, Joshua?"

"No, Clarence," Joshua said as the wide smile briefly disappeared from his face, but quickly returned.

"Are you sure?"

"Shaking his head vigorously up and down, Joshua responded, "Yes."

"Joshua, did you see anything that was strange or not normal the night your sister got hurt."

"No, Clarence."

At that point in the interrogation, Moore briefly stopped and was silent momentarily. He seemed to be unwilling to further question the impaired young man. *There is no way his testimony will be able to advance my investigation*, he thought. *I might as well wrap this up and proceed to the next sibling on my list.*

"Thank you, Joshua, for answering my questions," Moore said. He watched as Joshua arose from the kitchen chair and clumsily walked out to the living room. Moore felt sorry for the developmentally delayed boy with the unusually happy demeanor. His heart went out to him and to his family. After meeting Joshua, Moore felt more compelled to try to resolve the overriding question of who killed Rachael Miller.

Moore hoped that once he and Jean decided to have children that they wouldn't have to face a childhood genetic disorder. Moore realized at their current ages they would have an increased chance of having a less than perfect child. Nevertheless, if they did have a child with a disorder, God forbid, they would love the child anyway.

It was apparent that the Miller family had already paid a price most people shouldn't have to face with Joshua and now there was another crisis for them to be concerned with. Moore was sorry to have to question the family's character and integrity, but that's the job of a detective. He hoped the answers he was seeking would be forthcoming and quick for the family's sake. He liked the Millers, but that was not going to hinder him from doing his job.

Moore thought his interview with Joshua was necessary, but he felt Miller should have given him notice about his son's developmental issues. He realized that the Miller family had a far different view of Joshua than he did. To the Millers, Joshua seemed worthy to participate fully in life and he had well defined responsibilities as a family member. They knew his issues and accepted him as he was. To the family, he was a brother, a son, and an important person in their family, regardless of his issues

Moore noted down his thoughts on his legal pad and then referred to his suspect list. He paused for a moment and then asked Mrs. Miller if he could have another cup of tea. A few minutes later, a piping hot cup of Meadow tea was placed in front of him. Moore smiled at the woman and thanked her. He took a sip and said, "We can proceed.

I'd like to interview James next."

A few minutes later, a young Amish girl appeared in the kitchen. She said, "James is still doing some repairs in the chicken house. He asked if you could interview me first since he is in the process of fixing something mechanical."

"Sure, that's fine," Moore said. "What is your name and how old are you?"

"I'm Nora and I'm thirteen years-old," she said beaming.

Moore noticed she had brown hair and eyes like the rest of the family. She was smaller than Rachael at around eighty-five pounds. "My name is Detective Moore, nice to meet you."

"Nice to meet you too, Detective," she said politely.

"I am interviewing some of your family members with the hope of uncovering valuable information that might help me solve your sister's alleged homicide. I intend to ask you a series of questions and all you have to do is answer them. Can you do that for me?"

"Yes."

"Okay, let's begin. Did you and your sister get along well?"

"Yes."

"I assume you looked up to her, correct?"

"Yes."

"Nora, were you Rachael's best friend and did she confide in you?"

"What do you mean confide in me?" Nora asked innocently not fully understanding the meaning of the word.

"Did she tell you things; secret things that she had done or was doing?

"We were very good friends. I loved Rachael, but she never said much about her life. She was interested in my life though."

"I see. If you weren't her best friend, is there someone else in the family that was?"

"I'm not sure, but James was as close to being Rachael's best friend as anybody. Of course, she had girlfriends from school and I assume she told them things too."

"The night she died; did you see any unusual behavior from Rachael? Was she acting normal?"

"I think so. As I recall, she told me she was going to the barn to comb Dusty's mane."

"What time was that?" Moore asked hoping to learn more about the reason for Rachael's visit to the barn that evening.

"Well, it was about an hour or so after supper."

Moore glanced quickly over at Chilcott and gave him a meaningful look. Moore thought, *we've finally discovered the reason for her visit to the barn*. Or, *at least that is what she told her sister.* "Nora, did you see Rachael brushing her teeth, combing her hair, primping herself like she might have been expecting a visitor following supper."

"No, she did nothing like that. However, she did go back to her bedroom."

"Okay, did Rachael ever indicate she had a boyfriend she was secretly spending time with?"

"No; not that I am aware of."

"Were there ever any boys who came to visit her at home?"

"No, Mom and Dad would not allow it. She was only fifteen years old."

"Were you aware of anyone wanting to harm Rachael?"

"No."

"Nora, this is a very important question. Do you know anything about who might have killed Rachael?"

"No, Detective, I don't! But I hope you find the person responsible for her death and put them in jail."

"Me too, honey," Moore said. "I don't have any more questions. If you remember something important that happened, please tell your parents, so they can contact me. Thanks for your help."

Nora got up from the table and said, "You're welcome," and then left the kitchen."

Moore watched as the small child walked out of the room. She was dressed similar to Mrs. Miller and looked like a miniature image of her. He found Nora to be a very pleasant and sweet little girl. Unfortunately, she did not have much to add to help with the investigation. Moore thought, *dear Lord, I only need a small break to help me solve this juvenile's homicide. All it would take is a little divine intervention.* Moore didn't attend the Presbyterian church regularly, but he decided it would be a good idea for he and Jean to join a church in the future.

Chapter 10

Clarence Moore looked down at his wrist watch. He noted the time was 12:30 p.m. Moore wore a gold-plated Movado watch with a gold-plated metal band. When he glanced at the watch, the sight of it sometimes made him think about his late father, a person that he barely remembered. Largely because his father, Nathan Moore, died three years after Moore's birth. His mother Bessie saved the watch to give to Moore, when he turned eighteen just before joining the Army. After receiving the family heirloom from his mother, Moore took the watch to a local jeweler who refurbished it and made it look brand new.

Nora Miller had spoken with her older brother James at approximately 11:15 a.m. in the chicken coop. She told Detective Moore that James said he'd come to the kitchen to meet with Moore as soon as possible. But so far, James hadn't showed up. *Where is he?* Moore wondered. *It's been over an hour.* Moore was becoming more anxious and impatient as the minutes ticked by.

Jacob Miller stood up around 12:35 p.m. and said, "I'll go get him, Detective."

Moore replied, "Thank you very much. I appreciate your concern for my schedule."

"I'm sorry for the delay, but he gets to working on something and forgets what he is supposed to do next. He's still fairly young, Detective. You remember how you were at sixteen, I suppose. Boys at that age are irresponsible, flighty, immature, and prone to making misjudgments and mistakes."

"Yes, I do remember some irresponsible moments in my past," Moore reluctantly admitted.

"To be fair, I think we all remember those occasions that we would now want to avoid repeating," Miller said with a slight hint of concern on his face.

Through the process of elimination Moore had already deduced that James was the most likely suspect within the Miller family. The detective had plans to grill him harder than the rest. *But who knows for sure. Some of the Millers could be lying to protect their son or sibling. James might be trying to avoid the interview because he was fearful. Fearful that he might unwillingly admit responsibility for Rachael's death during the interrogation.* If that happened, Moore would arrest James, obtain his statement, and take him into custody. However, there could be risks associated with putting on a full court press. He'd learned in his basketball days that those types of presses can backfire on you if you're not careful. Sometimes, it's necessary to shake the bushes a little bit to get the desired answers from a suspect.

As Miller was going over these thoughts, the back door

slammed and James Miller appeared. He was greasy, sweaty, and looked as if he were put out. "Sorry for the delay Father, but the machinery is old and stubborn. It took me awhile to diagnosis the problem before I could fix it. It was a real pain, but I finally got it fixed," James said proudly as he hung up his heavy coat and Amish hat. "I'll wash my hands and be with you in a moment."

Three minutes later, James reappeared and sat down at the kitchen table across from Moore. The elder Miller introduced James to Detective Moore, as he had done with his other children.

"Are you here to tell us you found a lead to her killer, Detective?" James asked eagerly.

"No, but that's why I am doing lots of interviews to help me determine the facts in this case." Moore thought James Miller was an asshole for keeping him waiting for so long. "I have several questions that I would like you to answer."

"Okay Detective, ask away. I have nothing to hide," James said proudly.

The moment Moore heard James Miller volunteer that he had nothing to hide, the young man's words piqued his interest. *A statement like that could mean that the interviewee did have something to hide,* Moore thought. He looked across the table and nodded at Chilcott to turn on the recorder and place the microphone in front of the young Amish man.

Moore briefly observed James Miller before beginning the interview. He was rather striking for an Amish kid.

James looked to be over six-feet tall and was tanned. His hair was brown and more well-groomed than his siblings. James' large brown eyes boldly surveyed Moore. Moore could tell that James Miller thought he was special compared to his siblings. James appeared to have a sculptured physique, bedroom eyes, and an enticing and playful smile. Moore thought, *James would have no trouble attracting the attention of an interested, horny, and willing Amish girl.* If he was right about James, maybe Rachael had thought so too.

After a brief chat about life on the farm and other pleasantries with James, Moore felt James was very capable of carrying on a suggestive conversation with girls. James seemed very intelligent, but possibly manipulative, even though he only had an eighth-grade education. He wore an attractive long-sleeved flannel shirt with jeans. Moore had expected to see James wearing homemade broadfall pants with a plain-colored shirt, just like his brothers wore. The jeans were worn and soiled, but still looked half-way pressed and fit him well. He remembered the other boys' pants and shirts did not appear to fit as well as James' clothing did or were as stylish. Moore wondered how a young Amish kid could wear more stylish clothing than his siblings. But if he was in Rumspringa, he may have been wearing jeans, but would not have purchased them at an Amish store. Typically, Amish buy shirts, hats, socks, etc. at the Amish stores, but make their own pants. *Where did his money come from to buy fancy shirts and fancy jeans?*

Due to James' comment about not having anything to hide, Moore decided to Mirandize him, which he did prior to beginning his questioning. James Miller did not seem shaken by the Miranda warning. In fact, Moore felt James sensed that he might be considered a suspect. Moore stared briefly at his notes before starting the questions. "James," Moore began, "were you and Rachael close?"

"What do you mean by close, Detective?" Miller asked with a furrowed brow.

"Were you two best friends or soul mates, James?" Moore asked with a serious look on his face. "That's how your sister Nora described your relationship."

"Of course, Rachael and I were about the same age and we were brother and sister."

"Have you been involved in Rumspringa, since you turned sixteen?"

"Yes."

"Do you drink alcohol or do drugs?" Moore asked plainly.

"I've had some beers, but I've never done drugs," James replied.

"Alright, I'll move on then."

"You live at home, right? Moore inquired.

"Yes, and I have no intention of living outside the family home at the moment."

"I see," Moore said. "Why is that?"

"You need lots of money to either live with others or be on your own. I don't have that much money yet, Detective."

"Alright, I understand," Moore said shaking his head and smiling. "Have you ever been sexually active either before or after Rumspringa began?"

"Yes, I have. That's not a crime is it?"

"Well, that depends on the facts. Who have you slept with? Was she an older or younger woman?"

"What difference does that make, Detective?"

Moore looked over at the elder Miller and saw embarrassment and a touch of despair on his face the moment his son disclosed he was sexually active.

"Well, it depends on when it occurred. If you were younger than eighteen and an older woman, say twenty-two years-of-age or older offered her affection, even though it was consensual, the woman could be charged with statutory rape. Statutory rape in Ohio is a third-degree felony, which is punishable by at least one and up to five years in prison, and a fine of up to $10,000."

"Really! I had no idea about those things," James said with genuine surprise.

"Another example would be if someone like yourself, at age sixteen, has consensual sex with a person between the ages of thirteen and fifteen. That also could be a crime. Under the right set of circumstances sexual activity among minors may be construed as rape, particularly if the person engaged in the sexual activity knows that the other person is under sixteen. In Ohio, there is a statute that allows consensual sex between minors. It's called the Romeo and Juliet law. But if there is violence associated with the sexual activity between the two minors, it could be considered sexual battery, assault, or even murder. However, if the minors are siblings, the charge of incest might apply."

"That sounds very complicated," James stated plainly.

"Well, it all depends on several things and ultimately it's the prosecuting attorney's decision to make. At any rate, I would not want to be subject to the whims of a judge or prosecutor."

"I guess not," James said appearing a little edgy.

Moore knew he had not been completely honest or accurate about potential charges for sexual activity involving minors in Ohio. But he didn't have to be.

"Back to Rachael's case, are you aware of anyone who wanted to hurt or harm your sister?"

"No. Why would anyone want to do that to Rachael? She was well-liked by her peers and siblings. Rachael was cute, smart, friendly, and kind."

"James," Moore paused for effect, "did you know that Rachael has been sexually active too? Did you know that she had become pregnant recently and miscarried?" Moore looked deeply into James' big brown eyes and waited for a response from the obviously startled young man sitting across the table from him.

James Miller looked surprised and saddened to learn that Rachael had been pregnant and suffered a miscarriage. James said, "I had no idea about either of those things." He had a feeling from the way things were progressing that Detective Moore was going to ask him a very important question concerning Rachael's demise. James quickly tried to steel himself for the question.

Moore looked down at his notes and then looked James directly in the eyes. He wanted very much to see his reaction to the next question. Finally, he said, "Did you have sexual relations with your sister?"

"Absolutely not! How could you ask me such a question?"

Moore waited for a further response. There was none. Moore observed James shifting on his seat, looking downward, and to the right. He realized all these actions were indicative that James was lying.

"Son, if you tell me what happened that Monday evening in the barn with Rachael, it will go better for you."

"I've done nothing wrong, Detective. I would never hurt my sister or any of my siblings for that matter," James insisted.

"I think we should go down to my office at the Grant County Sheriff's Department and finish our discussion there. Is that alright with you, Mr. Miller?"

"No, I don't think so, Detective. Did you do it boy?" the elder Miller demanded.

"I've done nothing wrong, Father," James insisted.

"That's good enough for me, Detective. If the boy said he didn't do it then he didn't do it. I think you should leave right now," Miller said abruptly and stood up from the table.

"Jacob, I'd like to help your son, but this is going to make it harder for me to help. I hope you realize that," Moore said trying to encourage the Amish man to persuade his son to tell the authorities his side of the story.

"We'll see, Detective. Please gather your things and leave my house immediately," the elder Miller said firmly.

"I'll be happy to do as you have requested, but I think you should know that your son might be in serious trouble. If he wants to talk in the morning or you and your wife want to discuss this further with me, I am available to you at any time, day or night."

The elder Miller opened the back door and watched as the detectives left the house. On the drive back to the station, Moore indicated he was anxious to listen to the tape recording of his interrogation of James.

Chilcott asked, "So, do you believe James was having sex with Rachael and murdered her?"

"I have no idea at the present time what to believe. I'll need to listen to the tape carefully before I give you my opinion. *Maybe, I screwed up. Maybe, I should have tried to concentrate on getting him to admit he had sexual relations with Rachael first, before asking if he killed his sister. I'm fairly convinced his responses and manner during my questioning of him about having sexual relations with Rachael indicated he was lying to me. I'm sure they were sexually active, but I wonder if he knew she was pregnant or miscarried. What would be his motive to commit murder either way? Maybe her death was an accident?* "Randy, let's proceed with our plans to interview that teacher at Hillcrest Amish School tomorrow afternoon. Maybe she can shed some more light on this case. I doubt it, but we need to find out."

"Yeah, I think we should follow through on the lead," Chilcott commented. "All the information we can get, both on Rachael and James, will be helpful if there's a case to be made against James for possibly assaulting and murdering his sister."

"Yes, you're right about needing a lot of information about James in order to convict him of anything. If I understand Ohio law, James and Rachael could have had sex and neither one could be prosecuted. But if we can prove James is the presumed killer, of course, he would stand trial for the murder charge. Since he is a minor it would be up to the Prosecutor whether to charge James as an adult or as a minor. So, Randy, our job is to first determine who impregnated Rachael and then catch her probable killer. After that, we'll leave the rest for the prosecutor. Understand?"

"Yes, Boss," Chilcott said. "I do."

Chapter 11

Moore spent most of his time on Wednesday morning reviewing the known evidence, listening to the interrogation tapes of the Miller family members, and trying to make sense of the facts. He was fairly certain James Miller, Rachael's brother, was the father of her miscarried child. So, Moore decided it would be necessary to gather more evidence on him, but he was unsure what he'd do next. He was not convinced that James was the murderer. There was no apparent motive for him, and her death could have been accidental. But for the moment, James seemed to be the only likely suspect

The young man's comment concerning getting enough money was especially interesting to Moore and caught him off guard. *What did James mean by that statement? How was he going to get more money? After all, he was only sixteen and he'd been out of school for two years. Did he even have a paying job? Maybe he was hoping to sell drugs, steal, or do something else for cash. Was James that kind of person? He wondered how he could prove anything beyond a reasonable doubt. I don't think I can at this point. Maybe I should try to have him followed when he leaves the farm. But it would be hard since he lives in such a rural setting and uses a horse and buggy for transportation. He'd see he was being followed and that would raise his guard further.*

Moore thought, there was little or no reason to believe Rachael's other siblings were involved. However, he still wondered whether either Jacob or Sarah Miller had any idea that something was going on between their two children. If so, and depending on the circumstances, they could be charged with accessory and/or aiding and abetting a sexual battery, assault, childhood endangerment, or perhaps murder. *Maybe I will have to remind them of that possibility to help convince their son to come clean.* Moore hoped they'd convince their son to tell his side of the story to the authorities. And, as good and faithful Anabaptists, if the Millers were truly interested in their own salvation, honesty would be required. But Moore was not holding his breathe on that proposition.

The autopsy confirmed Rachael's death occurred as a result of the timber spike that almost completely severed her brain stem. The question was, did she fall back on it accidentally or did someone push her into it? Whether it occurred as an accidental shove or if it was intentional, it didn't matter. The act would still be serious and, at the very least, manslaughter or reckless homicide.

Dr. Peterson's forensic exam confirmed Rachael had been pregnant and subsequently miscarried several days prior to her death. The exam also indicated there was no appearance of rape, when she died. She could have been assaulted if the marks on her arms were caused by the fingers of an assailant pushing her back towards the post. But without a witness or confession, who could say what really happened for sure.

There were several finger prints on the flashlight. The state and federal authorities were searching their data bases for a match. There was a partial print on the outside back window of the barn near the site of the homicide. There were other prints taken inside the barn, and comparisons with the family member's prints were being performed.

The paper cup and lid found on the side of the barn were being examined for DNA evidence. The local laboratory confirmed there was a hint of rum and Coke still remaining in the container. There were no foot prints in the side yard leading from the road to the barn and back. And, there were no foot prints with traces of blood leading outside of the barn through the side door.

The urine test revealed that there were no drugs or alcohol in Rachael's system. There were no witnesses or evidence suggesting anyone other than a family member could have entered the barn between the hours of 6:00 and 9:00 p.m. on that Monday evening. It was believed Rachael was in the barn to groom her Shetland pony's mane.

There was evidence that on the following Tuesday morning Jonathan Miller entered the barn and discovered his deceased sister lying in a pool of her own blood. Following the discovery of the body, the entire family was confirmed to have entered the barn sometime around 4:40 a.m. Tuesday. Buggy tracks were visible in the Millers' driveway leaving and returning from Ted Johnson's home to the west, several miles from the Millers' house. Jonathan told Moore that he had phoned the Sheriff's Department from inside Johnson's residence. Johnson confirmed that fact. Jacob Miller said that he had instructed Jonathan to make a telephone call to the Grant County Sheriff's Department for help. No other tracks were found in the Millers' driveway.

However, one of the on-duty Deputy Sheriffs discovered a partial tire print on the access road to the corn field next to the Millers' barn. He photographed the print and made a plaster mold of it. Moore hoped there would be enough of an impression to identify the tire that made it, but he doubted it. Besides, he reasoned, it might have been made days before Rachael's demise and, therefore, would be irrelevant. The picture was sent to the State Police and the Federal Bureau of Investigation for identification purposes. The tire mold was also sent to the FBI.

Rachael's clothing was inspected and there were no signs of anything that shouldn't have been on her clothing. The blood samples on her coat and dress were being studied in the laboratory. The skin samples taken from inside of the coat's collar were identified as Rachael's.

Moore was conducting interviews to gather information concerning the possible homicide. And, he was waiting for various bits of information from the local, state, and federal law enforcement agencies involved. Moore understood it could be weeks to months before all those bits of evidence would be processed, developed, and returned to him. He wanted to be very thorough, but sometimes he got impatient.

Over the years, Moore developed some unsanctioned investigative and interrogation techniques that worked. The Chicago Police Department's unofficial policy was to allow some latitude with its detectives. But Moore recognized he was not in Chicago anymore. Grant County Sheriff Roger Jackson would never allow those things to happen in Grant County. Grant County was a very close-knit, conservative community and besides, Sheriff Jackson appreciated the distinction, authority, and financial rewards of the job.

Jackson was not going to jeopardize his long-term position as Sheriff and his pension on a case that might never be solved or might be referred back to the Amish Church community for resolution by the Grant County Prosecutor. Jackson was well aware of the Amish beliefs, religious tendencies, and long-standing practice of the authorities to allow the Amish to avoid the judicial system and settle the matter on their own terms.

Meanwhile, when Sergeant Randy Chilcott wasn't assisting Captain Moore with the Rachael Miller homicide investigation, he was busy working on the less serious criminal cases in Grant County. Those crimes involved automobile theft, drug dealing, and burglary for him to investigate, while Moore concentrated exclusively on the presumed case of homicide. Moore monitored Chilcott's investigatory progress and was pleased with the improvements, he was seeing. Captain Moore was aware that the prosecutor wanted the homicide case to be solved as soon as possible.

Captain Moore and Sheriff Jackson had been

summoned to meet with the prosecutor in his first-floor office located in the Grant County Courthouse. The courthouse was one of the oldest in Ohio and the structure was built before the start of the United States Civil War in 1858. The courthouse underwent an extensive remodeling effort in the early 1900's and then again in 1950. The administrative offices were housed on the main floor and the courts were located on the second floor. The courthouse, grounds, and facilities were well maintained despite their age.

Sheriff Roger Jackson was six-feet tall with dark brown hair and eyes. His blue uniform was spotless and neat. His shoes were black and spit-shined. He had been a police officer for the past thirty-five years in Wayne, Ohio and was elected fifteen years earlier as its Sheriff. Jackson was all business and everyone on the department staff knew it. Everything was done by the book. He'd received an associate's degree from the renowned Ohio State University in criminal justice and he excelled in his studies. Jackson graduated first in his class. He could have gone to work for a larger police department in communities the size of Columbus, Cleveland, or Cincinnati, but he chose to stay close to home. The citizens of Grant County didn't realize how lucky they were to have him serving in Wayne, Ohio. He was married, raised four grown children, and regularly attended the local Catholic Church, Saint Anthony of Padua. He, like Captain Moore, was a little concerned when the prosecutor's office called the meeting.

Samuel P. Murphy, the Grant County Prosecutor, had been around for so long that most folks forgot how many years he'd served. Murphy was sixty years-old and the twilight of his career was fast approaching. He also, like Jackson, was born and raised in the community of Wayne, Ohio. Murphy liked the small-town atmosphere and despised big cities. He didn't like the traffic, rude and impatient people, and the phony country club social gatherings prevalent in mostly larger cities, like Columbus for instance. He preferred the simple life with his wife Janice. They had been married for forty years. Murphy owned a two-story historic home near the outskirts of Wayne. He, like Jackson, ran his office by the book. There were no shenanigans played when it came to how he did his job.

Moore briefly met Murphy during his indoctrination period with the Sheriff's Department. Murphy was five-foot nine-inches tall, with salt and pepper hair, bushy white eye brows, and bright blue eyes. Murphy's pin-striped suit looked conservative and he was appropriately dressed for the position of Prosecutor. He looked the picture of health and enjoyed swimming daily in the summer and walking in the high school gymnasium during the winter. Moore could hardly believe the svelte-looking man was sixty. When he and Jackson entered Murphy's office, they received a respectful and pleasant greeting from him.

As Moore surveyed Murphy's office, he quickly noticed a dark mahogany desk and leather backed chairs. On the corner table in the office was a live plant. Countless legal books adorned the shelving. There also was a plaque identifying Murphy as a United States Army Korean War veteran next to the large book shelf. An honorable discharge certificate hung next to it along with a small framed Silver Star. The medal was awarded to Murphy for his service during the battle of Inchon. Murphy noticed Moore's interest in his award and accolades and asked, "Were you in the service, Detective?"

"Yes sir," Moore responded. "I was attached to an Army investigative unit of the military police. I served three years and was honorably discharged."

"You probably weren't aware that when you were hired to replace Tom Jacobs this past fall, Sheriff Jackson asked me for my input. I was impressed with your credentials and that you came from a family of law enforcement officers. Coming from Chicago, I'd guess you haven't been near as busy in Grant County. Is that correct?"

"Yes, that's correct and it's been a welcome change. I grew up six miles from the Loop and over the years that job wore me down. I appreciate life here more than I thought I would."

"Well, Clarence, that is why I asked Sheriff Jackson and yourself to come over so we could talk about the on-going case of the fifteen-year-old Amish girl's presumed homicide. As you'd probably imagine, Grant County does not get a homicide case that often. It's all people talk about in the restaurants and my friends and neighbors ask me how the case is progressing. I always tell them I can't talk about an on-going investigation, but I was wondering how things are going from your standpoint?" Murphy asked politely.

Moore turned toward Jackson, who was staring at Moore. Jackson was relieved the meeting did not concern a citizen complaint about his office. Jackson responded first by saying, “The case is only a week old. People can’t expect a quick and easy outcome this early. These investigations can take weeks and months to resolve. But Captain Moore has assured me that it is the only major case he is working on at the present time.”

“Good, I’m glad to hear that, Sheriff,” Murphy said with some relief. “Our constituents expect results and so do I.” Looking directly at Moore, Murphy asked, “Son, how do you think the investigation is progressing?”

“Truthfully sir, I am pleased with the investigation, thus far. We have accumulated some facts and have evidence in various forms being analyzed and processed by local, state, and federal law enforcement agencies. This case really involves two things. The first is to determine who impregnated Ms. Miller prior to her demise. The second phase will be to determine whether that person killed her. However, the evidence could suggest she accidentally died as a result of her own actions. But there is evidence which suggests she might have been assaulted and that could have caused or contributed to her death. There are a lot of factors to consider in this case. It will be difficult to unravel the truth, but I’ve got a lot of experience and a record of success in solving difficult criminal cases. I’m very hopeful about this case and I have developed a procedural plan to follow. So, I hope to figure out what really happened. It appears that there are no eye witnesses to the crime. Therefore, it will not be an easy case. I hope my comments have adequately answered your questions. I will keep you posted as things develop. But for the moment, the girl’s older brother, who I believe fathered the child, is the main suspect."

"Well, I've heard about that sort of thing, incest, I mean, occurring in the Amish community, but I have never prosecuted a case for it. But when a homicide is involved it is an entirely different matter. I feel sorry for the poor parents if what you believe is true. I think most all of the Amish are good and decent folks, but they do have different ways. But I suppose you've already found that out, haven't you?"

"Yes, that is true. People are mostly alike though, even in Chicago. But prior to taking this job I had no idea how much different the Amish are than those of us who they call the English or the non-Amish. It's really quite remarkable, sir," Moore said with a grin.

"I couldn't agree with you more, son," Murphy replied. "I'm looking forward to working with you. Thanks for taking time away from your busy schedule to give me an update. I can hardly wait for you to come through my door and tell me you've solved this case. Thanks for coming in and good luck."

Chapter 12

Following the meeting with Grant County Prosecutor Samuel Murphy, Moore and Chilcott planned to go to the Hillcrest Amish School. The school was located several miles from Jacob Miller's farm. Rachael was a recent graduate of the school and they were going there to interview Ms. Linda Hershberger, the teacher who taught Rachael Miller in the 8th grade.

Prior to going to the school, Chilcott invited Moore to eat lunch on his dime at Troyer's Café, his favorite restaurant in Wayne, Ohio. Mary Troyer's eatery was a household name in Wayne and her small diner was located inside a remodeled railroad car off Main St. Chilcott praised her cooking and the quantity of food she served ever since the first time he ate at her restaurant. Moore agreed to accompany him there for lunch. Normally, Moore's big meal was at night, but he told Chilcott he'd give it a try.

After they gorged themselves on a delicious Swiss steak dinner, Moore and Chilcott topped the meal off with a piece of apple pie a la mode. Within minutes, Moore wanted to take a nap. He'd eaten so much his stomach was bothering him. When Moore returned to the table from the restroom, the two detectives left the restaurant and pulled away in their unmarked police cruiser. School was not in session due to the Christmas holiday, but Chilcott told Moore he thought the teachers would be working at the school anyway. Upon their arrival at the two-room school house it was evident someone was inside.

The Hillcrest Amish School is a parochial school. It was built by the local Amish community to facilitate the education of their children. Rachael's former teacher, Linda Hershberger, was one of the teachers at the school. Hershberger was not that much older than the thirty-four Amish students she taught. She had no formal training in teaching and had not attended college or received an academic diploma in education. Regardless, she was a teacher for Hillcrest Amish School.

Amish schools teach grades 1 through 8. At age six, Amish children start first grade. The children are usually separated into two classrooms, grades 1 to 4 and grades 5 to 8. Ms. Hershberger taught grades 5 through 8. When school was in session, two older unmarried Amish women usually volunteered to be teaching assistants for the regular teachers. The main emphasis at the school was to teach reading, writing, and arithmetic. These are the skills that are needed to lead an Amish life and yet be able to do business in the outside world. The Amish students were called scholars and only attended classes through the eighth grade.

Schooling for Amish children is only part of the learning process necessary for preparation for the adult world. The structured learning programs for the children are supervised by their parents. The courses are conducted in English, and the children learn English at school. The curriculum for an Amish education is chosen by the school board with or without input from the teachers. All Amish school calendars mostly functions like public schools. Classes begin in August and conclude in May. Generally, the school year lasts for 180 days. Schools are the center of social activity from picnics to parent/teacher meetings to school programs. And, the parents take turns volunteering to serve on the local school board. The mission of an Amish education is to prepare children to remain Amish. In addition to reading, writing, and arithmetic, the school also teaches the value of hard work, community service, and obedience to the church.

When Chilcott arrived at the Hillcrest Amish School, Moore noticed a white wooden picket fence surrounding the grounds. The small, rectangular building with a chimney looked more like a small house than a school. It was constructed on the top of a small hill. There were several evergreen bushes outside in front of the building. The lot was partially covered with snow. There was a horse with a buggy tied up to what looked like a partially open-ended structure that served as a secure garage type building. The school building was painted white, stick-built, and occupied one level. There were two doors and several windows at the front and on the sides of the building. Playground equipment was visible on both sides of the lot. There was a swing gate at the entrance to the school and tying posts were available for ponies and horses. There was a small bathroom in the building for the boys and girls to use. A sink in a tiny kitchen area provided running water for the students to drink. There were several picnic tables outside adjacent to the school. A large stack of firewood was piled up on the left side of the yard. Moore envisioned a wood-burning stove located in the center of the room to provide heat. There were no electrical wires running to the building and Moore assumed the rooms were illuminated by kerosene lanterns.

Chilcott drove inside the grounds and parked near the strange looking open-ended garage. Inside the building, they could see two women cleaning. When the women noticed an automobile slowly approaching the school building, they quit cleaning and peered out the window. Moore supposed they received few visitors arriving in automobiles. The plain clothes officers got out of their white 1986 Ford LTD Crown Victoria and proceeded to the front door of the school. The two women dressed in Amish attire met them at the front door.

"Good afternoon, gentleman," the taller of the two young women said. "What can we do for you?"

"Good afternoon," Moore said flashing his police badge. "I'm Detective Moore and this is Detective Chilcott. We're from the Grant County Sheriff's Department. Are either of you ladies Linda Hershberger?"

The tall, plain-looking woman, who appeared to be in her early twenties, responded, "I'm Linda, what can I do for you?"

"Ms. Hershberger," Moore replied, "We are investigating Rachael Miller's death."

"How can I help?" Hershberger said immediately.

"Mrs. Miller informed me there were several older boys who attended school with Rachael. Supposedly one or both of them expressed an interest in dating Rachael. By any chance, would you know who those boys are? We'd like to interview them."

"Well, I don't, but let me think about it for a minute, Detective." Several seconds passed and Hershberger said, "Can you describe them?"

"No, unfortunately, I can't," Moore replied.

"Well, I've taught the 5th through 8th grade classes during the past several years. There were several young men in the 8th grade class, when Rachael was in 6th or 7th grade. Two in particular seemed interested in some of the younger girls in those classes. Rachael was a pretty girl, full of energy, smart, and very popular. In fact, I remember commenting to her folks that she maybe had too much personality. I'm sure she would have attracted their attention."

Moore thought that Hershberger's tone sounded critical and maybe even jealous of the deceased young woman. "Really," Moore replied. "Can you recall who those young men were?"

"Yes, I can. Their names are Nathan Yoder and LeRoy Swartzentruber."

"Do you know whether they still live in Grant County or have they moved away?"

"I think both were married within the last year. I heard

Yoder now lives in another Amish settlement a few counties away. Swartzentruber was killed in a bicycle/car accident on his way to work by a drunken driver several weeks after being married. It was a tragic accident. I felt so sorry for his wife."

"Oh, yes, I remember working that case," Chilcott interrupted. "It was a hit and run case. The driver didn't know he'd hit Swartzentruber until the following morning when he saw the dent in his car."

"Okay, thanks for your cooperation, Ms. Hershberger," Moore said. He felt slightly annoyed that Chilcott found it necessary to interrupt him. "That's all we need to know for now." *Looks as if that interview was another waste of time. It's doubtful that Nathan Yoder was involved in Rachael's death. But I'll have Chilcott check him out, regardless.*

A minute later, he and Chilcott were seated inside the Crown Victoria driving back to the Sheriff's Department. Moore decided to ignore Chilcott's rudeness for the time being. He announced to Chilcott that he would be doing some research for the rest of the afternoon. Specifically, Moore wanted to learn more about Rumspringa and what, if any part of the school curriculum, included sex education. Moore heard Deputy Sheriff Eugene Raber was raised in an Old Order Amish church, similar to Jacob Miller's church. Raber was one of the twenty percent of the Amish who do not return to their church community following Rumspringa. Of course, his parents disowned him and told him he was going to Hades when he failed to join their congregation. Nevertheless, Raber left home to pursue a new life with the English.

Upon Moore's return to his office, he asked the dispatcher to radio Deputy Sheriff Raber, who was on-duty. The message was 'Captain Moore wants to talk to you today as soon as possible," Raber was surprised by Moore's request, but he came back to the station and met Moore around 3:00 p.m. When Raber entered his office, Moore was taken aback by the height of the man. Eugene Raber was six-foot five-inches tall. He played in a local basketball league. When Raber heard that Moore was a former point guard on his high school and police league basketball teams in Chicago, he tried to recruit him for his team. Moore declined due to a persistent back injury sustained years earlier during a tussle with a dangerous criminal, while serving in the Chicago Police Department.

"Take a seat. Sergeant Raber," Captain Moore directed politely.

"What's this about?" Raber asked with a confused look on his face.

"I'm sure you're aware that I'm working on the Rachael Miller homicide case," Moore replied.

"Yes, it's all over the news, Captain."

"I was made aware that you were formerly Amish, prior to joining the Sheriff's Department."

"I was," Raber replied.

"Since I have no experience with the Amish, I hoped you'd help me understand several things about Rumspringa and sex education taught in the traditional Amish homes and schools."

"I can do that," Raber proclaimed. "Let's start with Rumspringa. I'll give you a brief overview of what it's all about."

"I hope you don't mind if I take a few notes, Sergeant," Moore said interrupting his subordinate.

"It's not that complicated, but go ahead and take notes if you want to," Raber said. "First, Rumspringa, which means 'running around', is marked by an increase in social activity. The term is used to describe the period adolescent Amish kids temporarily experience life differently. It starts at age 16. There are numerous myths about Rumspringa. Most Amish live at home as adolescents and do not live in the cities. Amish parents do not want their children to break the rules of the church. They want their children to behave morally. Rumspringa is not a time out from being Amish. Amish parents want their sons and daughters to live at home and attend church. The children are subject to community influences, although rules in the Ordnung may be bent and broken from time to time. Rumspringa is not a time to experiment with drugs, alcohol, or sex. Although, those things often occur when there is a wild and uncontrolled party."

"Very interesting," Moore commented. "Please continue, Sergeant."

"Rumspringa involves youth group participation in various social activities. Although, some are plainer and supervised, others are less conservative and are described as faster. In the case of faster, those groups tend to party more frequently and the parties occasionally get out of control. It's safe to say that the two different types are interspersed within Grant County's Amish communities. The plainer types play volleyball and have group singing events."

Raber continued, "Contrary to popular belief, most Amish do not participate in the faster types involving heavy partying, drug use, premarital sex, or other sinful behaviors. But those types of behavior do occur more frequently than the elder Amish would like to admit. Typically, Rumspringa ends after two years. But once a person marries, Rumspringa is over for good."

"Thank you, Sergeant. You've done a very good job explaining the concept," Moore exclaimed. "Now, if you would tell me about sexual education provided in the Amish schools, I would appreciate it."

"Before I tell you about that, I need to inform you about the personal understanding the Amish are taught concerning their gender. Girls are educated to be submissive to boys. Amish women stay at home; they're naïve and sheltered. They sew, perform daily chores, cook, clean, care for their children, do the gardening, and generally offer affection to their husbands on demand. Although a woman's place in Amish society may be submissive, her efforts are appreciated. But understand, wives are subordinate to their husbands."

Raber looked at Moore, who nodded at him to continue with his explanation. "Men are seen as the head of the household. The men tend to the farm and animals." Most men would consult with their wives about decisions, but then, the ultimate decision would be for them to decide. Gender relations within the Amish consist of an equal division of labor responsibility between the sexes. Men are also in charge of the spiritual life of the family and are responsible for providing sustenance."

"Can you tell me whether sex education is taught in the home or is it done in school?" Moore asked more specifically.

"For girls, growing up Amish limits their sexual information. Sex is infrequently talked about unless it's behind closed doors and with their mothers. Girls are prepared for menstruation, but discussing the reason for menstruation and the sexual act including foreplay is practically non-existent in most Old Order Amish homes. The schools teach relatively nothing about human sexuality or anatomy. Amish girls grow up in patriarchal households and have isolated lifestyles. Incest is blamed on women and they are victimized by a culture of victim shaming, if they are caught having illicit sex. There is little access to community justice or social awareness involving sexual activity. The Old Order Amish religion prioritizes repentance and forgiveness over punishment or rehabilitation."

Raber glanced at Moore to see if the captain wanted him to continue, and perceiving he did, Raber carried on. "Further, adults purposely ignore any mention of sex or sexual activity, especially in the presence of their children. Very little or no sex instruction is given to either the boys or the girls in the typical Amish home. The youth learn about the birds and the bees informally. Gradually, Amish children begin to understand sexuality, piece by piece, by watching the sexual behavior of their farm animals. Often, children will discuss sex in private conversations with their peers and older siblings. The use of condoms is forbidden by the church, but protected sex is practiced."

"Well, that's about it," Raber concluded. "If you want more information there are books in the library that discuss the Amish lifestyle."

"Oh, I don't think that is necessary. You have provided the answers to most of my questions regarding the Amish. Thank you so much for your help, Sergeant Raber." Moore patted Raber on the shoulder appreciatively and shook his hand as he departed Moore's office. *Finally, I think I have the knowledge necessary to understand these people better. Hopefully, that knowledge can be used to solve this case.*

Chapter 13

The drive from Lake James, Indiana to the Grant County Community Hospital in Wayne, Ohio took Dr. William Peterson a little over an hour. He maintained a small, inexpensive apartment in Wayne and stayed there during the week and sometimes on weekends. His presence in Wayne was dictated by his work schedule.

Peterson also owned a year-round home on Lake James, where he grew up. The maroon 1986 Mercedes Benz sedan that he drove was a dependable vehicle in snow, ice, and in hazardous conditions. Peterson purchased snow tires for the vehicle and the car handled wonderfully during the winter. He didn't have to work over the weekend and was returning to Wayne early in the morning. When he arrived at the hospital it was 6:45 a.m. on Monday, January 2, 1989. His shift started at 7:00 a.m.

Dr. Peterson walked into the hospital and entered the secure and private corridor leading to his first-floor office. He hung up his overcoat and sat down at his desk. Peterson's least favorite task was to assemble the medical reports and forms, required for each patient he'd treated into a file folder. He also was responsible for reviewing and gathering the paperwork on the deceased people he'd autopsied. As he placed the medical reports into each individual file folder, he checked to make sure the proper paperwork was included and complete.

When he began to review Rachael Miller's medical records, he was shocked to see the urine analysis section contained no conclusion concerning the alcohol and drug testing that was supposed to be performed. There was an order form in the file that he signed to authorize the test. Normally, the urine analysis report would highlight all the findings concerning the patient's urine, but there were no comments in the appropriate section on drugs or alcohol. He recalled submitting the order. And, he remembered Barney Yoder telling him there was no indication of alcohol or drugs present in the Amish girl's system. Apparently, the results of the test were never recorded for some reason. *I wonder if Barney forgot to do the test and assumed nothing was wrong. After all, who would expect a fifteen-year-old Amish girl to test positive for drugs?*

Immediately, Dr. Peterson called the front information desk and asked for Barney Yoder to be paged. The message was that Dr. Peterson wants to see you in his office as soon as possible. Peterson was working on compiling another file folder when he heard a knock on his office door. He looked up and saw Yoder through the clear glass in the door and motioned for him to come in.

"What can I do for you, Dr. Peterson?" Yoder asked apprehensively upon entering the physician's sterile looking professional office. He was concerned because Peterson had never summoned him to come to his office that early in the morning.

"Well, I was reviewing the medical reports on Rachael Miller, the young Amish girl that was killed about two weeks ago. You remember her, don't you?"

"Yes, I remember her," Yoder replied.

"I've uncovered a discrepancy in one of the reports; specifically, the urine analysis. I distinctly remember you telling Paul and me that the girl's system tested negative for alcohol and drugs. Do you remember saying that?"

"Yes, the laboratory technician told me she was clean, meaning there was no indication of alcohol or drugs in her system."

"Could you have misunderstood her, or gotten it wrong?" Peterson asked with a serious tone and a questioning look on his face.

"No, I specifically remember she told me the girl was clean of drugs and alcohol in her system."

"Are you sure, Barney?"

"Yes, I am, Doc."

"Well, I'm going to take your word for it. Unfortunately, I'll have to tell the Coroner about the discrepancy and order another urine test to be done. Would you provide the laboratory with another sample from her urine stored in the evidence container inside the morgue? Tell them to redo the test, and return their written results to me, as soon as possible."

Yoder complied with Dr. Peterson's request. He knew

from experience that urine tests are normally used to measure THC levels in a person's system. Alcohol would be done in the same manner, but after two weeks the result would probably be inconclusive.

Yoder also knew that THC levels can be detected in a person for up to 30 days, particularly if the person was more than a one-time user. However, Yoder thought, THC typically dissipates in a couple of weeks. Rachael had been dead a little over two weeks. *I wonder if it's possible to record a valid test result after so long? The time it takes your body to get rid of THC depends on your metabolic rate, your hydration, your weight, and the amount of fat cells in your body. Rachael Miller was not overweight and she appeared to be physically fit.* Yoder remembered that he'd heard Dr. Peterson say that women have more fat cells than men, so maybe her gender might offer a wider window than average.

Peterson also made another call following his meeting with Barney Yoder. The physician decided to contact the hospital laboratory supervisor. The supervising nurse responsible for laboratory operations in the hospital was RN Betty Johnson. She seemed to be a likable person, but Peterson thought she acted rather dipsy. He wondered if she was all that proficient in regards to running the laboratory. At the very least, Peterson wanted to ensure this type of thing never happened again, and secondly, he wanted the person responsible for failing to conduct the test to be written up. Johnson assured him it wouldn't happen again and promised to speak to the technician responsible for the error. Her carefully worded apology and response appeased Dr. Peterson.

Before 9:00 a.m., Yoder returned to Peterson's office with a new report in a sealed manila hospital envelope. He handed the envelope to Peterson and quickly left his office. There was no "thank you Barney" in Peterson's response. His comment was "finally" as he grabbed the report out of the long-time hospital employee's hands and returned to his desk. Dr. Peterson had a reputation of sometimes being abrasive, callous, and rude. Yoder didn't want to be on the receiving end of the doctor's wrath.

Upon studying the report, Peterson found there were small levels of THC in Rachael's system. *God damn it, he thought.* He noted the alcohol content was still not recorded. The pathologist also considered testing a sample of Rachael's hair or to do a blood test as backup to the urine test, but decided it was not necessary. This time, he was sure the test was done and accurately. He wondered whether Nurse Johnson conducted the test herself.

It was common knowledge around the hospital that Dr. William Peterson was a perfectionist and that he hated mistakes. The staff was happy to have such a highly-rated pathologist on their staff, but the hospital director knew he had some attitude issues. He could be tough to work with, particularly if the staff performed unprofessionally and poorly. Donald Wysong, the hospital director, didn't want to broach the subject with Dr. Peterson for fear that he might be opening a can of worms.

* * *

Detective Moore received a message from Jacob Miller, while Moore was in the men's room. Apparently, the Amish man called the Sheriff's Department and asked to talk to Detective Moore. When Moore failed to answer the call, Miller chose to leave a message that he wanted to talk to Detective Moore as soon as possible. Moore was cautiously optimistic as he hurried to his unmarked vehicle and drove to Miller's farm on County Road W200S. Chilcott had taken a personal day off on December 2, 1988. So, Moore picked up the recorder and microphone off Chilcott's desk on his way out the door. Most of the snow was melting and there were spots of moisture still remaining on the pavement.

Twenty minutes later, Moore pulled into Jacob and Sarah Miller's driveway. He parked the car and approached the back door. Upon seeing Moore in the driveway Jacob Miller opened the back door and met him as he was approaching the sidewalk. "I understand you wanted to talk to me," Moore said guardedly as he extended his arm to shake the man's hand.

Miller shook his hand and said, "Yes, I do." Moore noticed Miller had a look of despair on his face when he spoke.

"I wanted to clear something up that was talked about during your interview with my son James this past Tuesday afternoon. Apparently, James did not tell you the truth. After I requested you leave my home, I talked to Jonathan. I questioned him about several things. Anyway, James told you he had never done drugs before, but Jonathan confirmed that he lied. He told me he'd seen his brother smoke marijuana several times. Jonathan claimed that James told him he kept a supply of it in the barn. Jonathan and I searched the barn and found a small bag of marijuana hidden in the hayloft. I took it, set the marijuana on fire, and confronted James about it. James told me the bag I destroyed was his. Obviously, he no longer has it in his possession. I just wanted you to know that Jacob Miller is an honest man, even if his son is not."

Moore was shocked that both Jacob and Jonathan Miller snitched on James. The knowledge about Jacob's son's drug use was interesting. But without the evidence there could be no prosecution of James for possession. Moore hoped Miller would talk to his son and seek help for his drug problem. *There was no reason to have another bad situation affect his family. They had enough on their plate as it was,* Moore thought.

"I appreciate you telling me the truth," Detective Moore said. "It's rarely ever done, Jacob. With that in mind, would you reconsider allowing me to interview James again? I had some more questions for him that were left unanswered?"

Miller briefly contemplated Moore's request before responding. "I'd like to talk to Sarah about your request before I make that decision. Let me think about it for a few days. I'll contact you on Thursday morning."

Moore was surprised by the elder Miller's announcement and cautiously optimistic about his chances to get a second opportunity to interrogate James. Perhaps he wouldn't need to provide cause to a judge for a warrant. If Miller allowed the second interview to occur, he could bring up the potential charges that could be levied against his parents, if James was proven to be guilty of murder. It was the perfect scenario, as long as Miller didn't decide to hire an attorney. Moore thanked Miller for his honesty and for being an honorable man. The Amish man shook Moore's hand, and then watched as Moore returned to his vehicle and drove away.

Moore was delighted that Miller didn't close the door on his request to do a second interview with his son. If given the chance to interview James again, he thought he would proceed differently. Moore decided he would press James on the notion that he was having illicit sex with his sister Rachael. If James admitted that, Moore was sure Mr. Miller would allow him to press further on whether or not he'd possibly killed her. The question of motive still haunted him. What possible reason could there be for James to kill Rachael?

The following morning, Moore would receive a facsimile from the Grant County Community Hospital that would provide information that could indicate a possible motive.

Chapter 14

Moore took a half-day off from work on Monday afternoon to spend time with his wife, Jean. She seemed to be working almost 24-7. Clarence knew he was preoccupied trying to solve the presumed murder case of Rachael Miller. They both thought their current work schedules were negatively affecting their marriage. Moore felt like they were two ships at sea, passing each other at night, as they pursued their various responsibilities.

Jean expressed interest in seeing a movie on the big screen and wanting to try a five-star restaurant she'd discovered in a Toledo, Ohio tourist magazine. They both felt like they needed time to reconnect, have some fun, and reignite their normally passionate sex life. When they lived in Chicago, all those things could be accomplished at the end of the work day. Chicago offered close, countless opportunities for entertainment and socializing. But living in rural Grant County made it more difficult to do fun things. Of course, they realized there were pluses and minuses associated with any relocation. So far, they were happy with the move.

Unfortunately, when the couple arrived at The Hoof

and Claw Restaurant, they were disappointed to find out the restaurant was closed on Mondays. Nevertheless, they had a good steak and lobster dinner at a chain steakhouse near the outskirts of Toledo. After the meal, Moore managed to find a local cinema two blocks from downtown. The Alan Theater was locally owned and operated. There were five top-rated movies playing at the theater. They were: The Accused, starring Jodie Foster, Mississippi Burning, starring Gene Hackman, Working Girls, starring Melanie Griffith, Cocktail, starring Tom Cruise, and Rain Man, starring Cruise and Dustin Hoffman. They picked Rain Man and purchased a large box of buttered popcorn with Cokes to enjoy during the movie.

On the return trip back to Hancock Lake, they decided it was a good idea to get away more frequently. Neither Clarence nor Jean discussed work during the evening and they both admitted they felt like they'd had a wonderful outing. After parking Jean's company car in the driveway, Moore unlocked the back door to their newly constructed A-frame and they went inside. Clarence lit the gas logs in the fireplace, while Jean made each of them a cocktail. Before cuddling up to Clarence on the couch, Jean turned on some romantic music and they enjoyed the orange and blue colored flames, the music, casual conversation, and an occasional kiss.

After about an hour, Clarence turned off the gas log and they climbed the steps to their second-floor suite. To Clarence's delight, Jean provided a slow, erotic, and playful strip tease as she slowly removed her clothing. Clarence practically ripped his clothes off after seeing her naked form. Jean slid under the bed covers first followed quickly by Clarence, who made impassioned love to her for almost an hour.

The following morning, Clarence prepared a delicious bacon, cheese, and onion omelet for them to eat. At 7:00 a.m. Clarence was out the door and Jean was almost ready to leave for her appointment in Ft. Wayne, Indiana, as well. Moore pulled into the Sheriff's Department parking lot just before 7:30 a.m. He got out of his car and headed for the employee lounge, where he made a cup of hot tea. On the way to his office, he stopped by Chilcott's desk and instructed him to look into Nathan Yoder's record. Moore reminded Chilcott that Yoder was now supposedly residing several counties away.

When Moore returned to his office, he reminded himself that he should thank Deputy Sheriff Raber again for his help concerning Rumspringa and how the Amish children are educated about sex. Moore sat down behind his desk, but found himself reflecting on the prior evening. *We should do that every few weeks*, he thought. Sipping on his piping hot tea, Clarence reminded himself it was time to concentrate on the Miller case and get it solved. He was expecting evidence to slowly start trickling in and he knew it was a just matter of time before he'd get the break he was looking for. Moore didn't notice the rolled-up facsimile in his in-box on top of his credenza. For the next two hours, he was consumed with reading through the prior day's criminal incident reports. When he finished reviewing the reports, he got up and made another cup of tea, and then shared the reports with Sergeant Chilcott.

Upon returning to his office, he noticed a departmental letter from the Sheriff that had been placed in his in-box. He retrieved the routine memo and noticed the rolled-up facsimile in his basket. He grabbed both the memo and the facsimile and placed them on his desk. Moore unrolled the facsimile first and discovered it was from the Coroner's office. As he read the short notice, Moore quickly realized the information enclosed might end up being his first real break in the Miller case. The facsimile read, "To: Detective Clarence Moore, Grant County Sheriff's Department. In regards to the Rachael Miller homicide investigation, please note there is a change in the urine analysis report for Ms. Miller, the deceased. The original autopsy indicated no THC present in Miller's system at the time of her death. However, due to a discrepancy in our testing, our current analysis indicates there was THC in the deceased girls system. We are sorry for providing you with inaccurate information on the autopsy report. If you need further information or clarification, don't hesitate to call Dr. William Peterson at the Grant County Community Hospital. The report was signed by Paul Smith, Coroner for Grant County, Ohio."

Moore was extremely excited. Now, there was a possible explanation as to why James and Rachael became sexually involved. Of course, they might have just wanted to experiment with their own sexuality. From investigating past cases involving marijuana use, Moore knew that ingesting THC can alter senses, change moods, and affect rational thinking. He imagined sexual interest between brother and sister could have been enhanced by THC use. The siblings were young, not well-educated, immature, and naïve. He thought James probably provided Rachael with the opportunity to experience marijuana discreetly. He also wondered whether James might be the source for marijuana use by other Amish kids going through Rumspringa. Maybe that was how he obtained the extra money he mentioned in his earlier testimony.

Maybe, after James and Rachael smoked some pot, things that had been previously considered taboo might have come to fruition. Maybe they temporarily lost control of their emotions and experimented with sex. Moore could imagine James telling his sister, who better to have sex with than your brother. James was shrewd enough to convince Rachael that nobody would know and nobody would get hurt. After all, the two of them were best friends and soul mates.

Moore wondered whether Rachael and James might have gotten into a small tussle over her reluctance to provide sexual favors on that fateful Monday evening, especially since she had been pregnant and miscarried. James could have gotten overwhelmed with the situation, and out of anger, accidentally pushed her into the spike. After realizing what he'd done, James might have fled the barn and kept his mouth shut.

Moore thought, *I've developed a scenario with a possible motive for manslaughter.* But he could not be sure without a confession from the immature and arrogant son of Jacob Miller. He hoped the elder Miller would give him the opportunity to talk to James without the need of obtaining a warrant. If so, Moore planned to concentrate on getting him to confess to having sexual relations with

Rachael before bringing up his possible role in the presumed homicide.

Minutes later, he told Chilcott that Rachael was confirmed to have THC in her system. He also updated Chilcott about Jacob Miller confirming that James used marijuana as well.

Chilcott commented, "Well, I guess we can assume that James must have shared the weed with his sister."

"I wonder who is providing the marijuana to James," Moore replied.

"I, uh, wouldn't know and I doubt if we'll ever find that out. The kid will probably keep his mouth shut for fear of repercussions from the dealer." Chilcott thought, *I hope that Amish kid doesn't tell Moore where he got the weed. If Monica was thought to be involved, the authorities would accuse me. And, if they could prove my participation, I'd lose my job, go to jail, and my life would be ruined.*

"Well, don't be too sure about that. I've been fairly successful over the years getting kids like James to spill the beans."

"I'm sure you have," Chilcott responded. "But remember, these Amish are very stubborn." *He hoped James remembered the warning Monica gave him. Just because he was Amish didn't mean he was stupid.*

"I think I can handle James," Moore said with a grin.

"We'll see, Captain," Chilcott responded blankly.

Moore was surprised that Chilcott didn't seem at all excited about the revelation. He was puzzled. Maybe

Chilcott was having a bad day. He'd heard from one of Chilcott's best friends in the Department that Chilcott's relationship with his girlfriend, Monica Kerlin, was faltering. Moore had asked Chilcott about it several days earlier. Chilcott said they were working on it. Moore wondered whether the young couple was having second thoughts about marriage.

Moore asked, "Did you get things worked out with Monica?" Judging from Chilcott's mood, he was not expecting a positive answer.

"Well, I guess I'll tell you the truth," Chilcott said. "We are taking a break from our relationship. Monica left yesterday afternoon to move into her mother's house."

"What does that mean?" Moore asked. "How long will she be gone?"

"She left the car in the garage and only took a handful of clothes, so I don't know. I took her to the bus station, gave her a wad of cash, and dropped her off. I left right after she got out of the car. I couldn't stand seeing her leave. She knows I love her, but maybe she isn't ready to commit. I have no idea when she'll return." *Knowing the fact that she'd never return consoled Chilcott.*

"Randy, I'm so sorry to hear Monica left you," Moore replied sincerely.

"Thanks boss, I'm praying she'll be back, but I don't know if she thinks she has a reason to return. I bought the car for her, but it's titled in my name. I paid for most of her clothes. She only left a few personal items, so I just don't know how she's feeling about the future of our relationship."

"Is there anything I can do for you? Would you like to take a few days off, pay her a visit, and talk to her?" Moore offered.

"Nah, but thanks anyway, Captain. I'd prefer to stay busy at work rather than sitting around the house and moping about it."

"Okay, Randy. Suit yourself, but if you change your mind, come and see me."

"Thanks, I appreciate your concern, Boss," said Chilcott knowing full-well that Monica Kerlin would be next to impossible to find.

Chapter 15

After Moore left Chilcott's office, Chilcott began to relive what happened to him during the New Year's weekend. He had taken Monica out to dinner at a fancy restaurant on New Year's Eve and they enjoyed a good meal. Later, he remembered stopping at his favorite tavern and drinking too many cocktails. By the time he drove the police car into his garage, it was apparent the two of them were intoxicated to varying degrees. Monica could barely walk into the house and she was almost falling-down drunk.

When the crystal ball fell in Times Square on their television set at Midnight, they toasted each other with champagne. Following the traditional kiss and another glass of champagne, Monica said to him out of the blue slurring her words, "You know, you should appreciate me a little more than yah do. Yes, you should. You should," she said repeating herself with less and less enthusiasm.

Chilcott replied, "You know, I appreciate you, yeah so much, sweetheart!" Saliva and champagne ran down the side of his mouth as he spoke.

"Hey, I'm serious, asshole," she blurted in a boozy slur. "My sales are really payin'. Yeah, you heard me, payin'. I'm makin' real cash."

Chilcott tried to focus to understand Monica's slurred gibberish, but he was getting annoyed. "Yeah, as long as I don't put your sweet ass in jail, you might be makin' money." Chilcott replied slobbering as he spoke.

"You wouldn't arrest me. Who else would screw your brains out, darlin'?"

"Yeah, yeah," he said. "But don't be too sure about yourself, honey."

"Oh yeah! Well, don't piss me off, or there'd be no cash in it for you either. And if you tried to rat on me, I'll tell your Boss, that Captain Morgan, or whatever his name is," she said sounding threatening, despite swaying drunkenly.

"What would you tell him?" Chilcott's tone also sounded more seriously threatening.

"That I got cash from you to buy weed," she said and then gave him the finger.

"Seriously? You'd never do that, would you?" Chilcott's eyes were glazed and his words were getting more slurred. "I'll lose my job and go to jail!"

"I would!" Monica shouted.

"You're not really serious, are you?" He asked again.

"I'm one hundred percent serious, if you try messin' with me. You do, and you're gonna be sorry."

Chilcott thought briefly about what she threatened to do

and excused himself. He told her, "We'll resume this conversation after I take a leak." He walked outside, unzipped and took a piss standing behind a tree. That helped him feel a little bit more sober, but even more pissed off at Monica. *Who the hell does she think she is threatening me, the little bitch!?*

When he reentered the house, he held a 25-caliber hand gun with a silencer attached.

Monica realized she'd probably gone too far, but was sure her fiancé was just trying to scare her. So, when Chilcott pointed the gun in her direction, she laughed and said, "You don't have the balls to pull the trigger, you stupid piece of shit. I'm only with your dumb ass, because I have nowheres else to go." She burped, then added, "That's why I'm sellin' weed, to get the hell out of here."

Two seconds later, a 25-caliber projectile blasted into her chest. Blood slowly began to ooze out onto her blouse. She blinked and then collapsed on the living room floor. *I must have hit her directly in the heart.* He felt for a pulse. There was an irregular, but shallow beat. Chilcott bent down, put the tip of the silencer on her temple, and fired two bullets into her brain. *That should do the job.*

He sat on the couch for several minutes. His mind buzzed and refused to focus. Finally, he asked himself out loud, "What I am going to do next? Chilcott didn't feel panicky. As his mind became clearer, he began to think about what he should do with the body.

He shook his head, got up, walked out to the garage, grabbed a black plastic tarp, and a roll of duct tape. Then, he placed her body on top of the tarp and rolled her up inside it. He secured the tarp and the corpse with duct tape and carried the body out to the Oldsmobile parked in the garage. Chilcott placed a strip of plastic sheeting inside the trunk of the car to protect the carpeted floor from any spillage of blood. He grabbed a shovel and a pick and placed them and the body in the trunk and closed the lid.

Chilcott returned to the house with a bucket of water, a stiff brush, a sponge, several rags, and a gallon of bleach. It took several hours of scrubbing and cleaning to rid the wooden floor of the blood splatter. He cleaned blood off his shoes, the bloody foot prints on the floor, and then rinsed and cleaned the bucket several times with hot soapy water. He went outside and burned the rags and the sponge in his fire pit and returned to the house. Afterwards, he took a quick shower, loaded up the washing machine with his blood-stained clothes, and went to bed.

Early in the morning, he got up, ate a light breakfast, and had several cups of coffee before driving away in the 1983 Oldsmobile Cutlass. Chilcott noticed the fuel gauge was almost on empty, so he stopped at his favorite Sunoco gas station in Wayne to fill up the tank. An hour later, he was on I-75 heading south. Traffic was light and Chilcott was making good time. He was careful to keep his speed just under the speed limit. He refueled once again in southern Ohio, just before entering into Kentucky. Chilcott planned to get rid of the body at least six hours away from Wayne. He hadn't decided exactly where, but thought he'd bury her just inside the Tennessee line right off of the turnpike.

After crossing the Tennessee line and after driving about fifteen more minutes, Chilcott saw a small sign on the side of the road indicating there was a tourist attraction ahead. The sign read, 'Hiking Trails and Overlook Site'. So, he slowed down and pulled off the roadway by the sign. He turned onto a narrow gravel road. Chilcott drove a short distance and then noticed a clearing off to the right side of the road. It was located near the trailhead of a hiking path. The sun was going down as he backed the car into the clearing. There appeared to be no one around the area. He hoped no one would show up, otherwise, he thought, *I might have to deal with them too.*

Chilcott sat in the car and waited and watched for a few minutes before he got out of the car and removed the shovel and pick from the trunk. He noticed that the woods was pretty dense along the trail. Chilcott walked beyond the trailhead and then fifty paces off the trail into the woods, where he found a secluded spot for the grave. The ground was fairly hard as the soil was a combination of dirt and small pieces of rock. It took him twenty minutes to dig down far enough to make a suitable grave.

Chilcott returned to the Olds with the pick, but left the shovel by the hole he'd dug. He placed the pick back inside the trunk, and then retrieved the corpse wrapped in plastic. He threw the burden over his shoulder and carried it back to the freshly dug grave. He laid Monica carefully into the hole. He shoveled enough dirt to cover her, and then placed small fallen branches and leaves over the grave. He paused momentarily for a brief goodbye, and then carried the shovel back to the car. Chilcott placed the shovel inside the trunk and closed the lid. He slid onto the clothe-covered padded car seat and drove away.

About two hours later, he pulled off I-75 to refuel, grab a soft drink, and go to the restroom. Due to heavy holiday traffic, it was well-past midnight when he arrived home. When he opened the trunk to remove his tools, he smelled a slight noxious odor. Chilcott grabbed an aerosol can of Lysol from his work bench and sprayed a generous amount inside the trunk. He decided it would be wise to leave the trunk lid up for a day or two to air it out.

In the morning, he awoke early as usual, ate a light breakfast, gulped down some coffee, took a quick shower, and was at his desk before Moore arrived for work at 7:30 a.m. Chilcott was certain he'd thought of everything.

When Chilcott returned home after work, he removed the small piece of plastic sheeting from the trunk. He noticed a bit of blood on it. He looked, but didn't see any additional blood on the carpeted floor or outside on the exterior of the vehicle. Chilcott burned the small plastic sheeting in his burn pit and went inside to make supper. He failed to remove the hand gun that was secured under the driver's seat.

Chapter 16

In response to Moore's request for a second interview of James Miller, Jacob Miller promised he would call Moore at the Sheriff's Department on Thursday morning. So, Moore made sure he was at his desk to receive Miller's telephone call at 7:30 a.m. When Moore's office phone rang just after 9:00 a.m., he quickly picked up the receiver and said, "Detective Moore speaking." He was pleased to hear the voice of Jacob Miller say, "Hello Detective, this is Jacob Miller calling."

There was a pause and then Miller continued, "The wife and I discussed whether or not we would allow you to meet with James again."

Moore was hanging on his every word, anxiously waiting for the response to his request. In a barely controlled voice, Moore asked, "What did you decide to do, Jacob?"

"We're willing to let you interview our son again. However, I want you to conduct the interview outside of our home. I'll bring him to the Sheriff's Department if you want, but I don't want you to come back to our house and take him away in your police car." Miller said firmly.

"I'm more than willing to come back to your home and interview him there." Moore replied.

"No, both the wife and I are disappointed in the boy and we don't appreciate being lied too. Besides, we don't want the other children to know what's happening. Nevertheless, I want to be with him during your interrogation."

Moore was delighted with the Millers' decision. It was exactly what he'd hoped for, but didn't expect. On reflection, he realized it was Jacob Miller's way of sheltering the rest of the family from James' sins and failures. Moore thought it was probably a good decision for Jacob's family. He also thought that Miller probably didn't realize how serious the trouble was that his son might be in. *Just because Jacob had destroyed the marijuana didn't mean that James was clear of any drug charges. We might not have the physical evidence to charge James with possession,* Moore thought. *If a witness comes forward to testify that James sold drugs to others, he could face the more serious charge of dealing. And, James was still a suspect in his sister's possible homicide. He might have accidentally killed Rachael in a dispute over pot. Whatever James' role was, intentional, accidental, or none at all, Moore was determined to find that out in his next interview.*

"When do you want to interview him?" Miller asked. "I could bring him in tomorrow morning, if that would work for you?"

"Yes, that will work for me." Moore said. "Anytime in the morning would be fine. My shift starts at 8:00 a.m." He thought for a moment, and said, "How about 9:00 a.m.?"

"How long do you think the interview will take?"

"Well, that really depends on how readily your son cooperates with us. It could range from an hour to longer," Moore replied. He realized that Miller had little or no understanding about what might occur during the interrogation. After all, Miller only believed his son had tried marijuana and nothing more. If he admitted to having sex with Rachael, being a dealer, or murderer, well... things could go from bad to worse for the young Amish man. James would be arrested and held in jail, unless he was bailed out, until a trial was held. Of course, he could walk away still a free man. It all depended on his testimony, the available evidence, and whether or not he was a credible witness for himself.

* * *

The next day at 9:00 a.m., Jacob Miller arrived with his son, James, at the Grant County Sheriff's Department for questioning. When they were escorted into the interrogation room, both James and Jacob noticed a video recording device mounted in the far, top corner of the room. Sergeant Chilcott and Captain Moore were waiting for them in the room.

As soon as the two Amish men were escorted into the room, Captain Moore asked the elder Miller if it was alright to record the interview. Jacob reluctantly consented. Moore then gestured toward two of the four chairs at the rectangular table in the center of the room inviting the Millers to take a seat at the table next to each other. Moore and Chilcott seated themselves on the opposite side of the table from the Amish men. Moore had a stack of papers, a lined, legal-sized white pad, and a pen sitting in front of him. Sheriff Jackson was in the observation room watching and waiting for the interrogation to begin.

Moore gave the standard Miranda warning to James. He carefully asked whether James understood its meaning. James affirmed that he understood. Moore began the interview by indicating that he might ask some of the same questions he'd asked James during the first interview.

"That's fine with me," James replied. "I'm here to truthfully answer all your questions, Detective." The young man appeared different than when they'd first met in the Miller home. His head hung forward and he looked dejected. Moore thought the elder Miller must have had a "Come to Jesus talk" with his son. He assumed the elder Miller demanded respect in the family and when he didn't get it there were consequences.

Moore looked directly at James and asked, "Do you want to change your testimony about any of the answers you gave during our first interview?"

"Yes, Detective, I do," James replied. "I told you I didn't use drugs or have them in my possession. I lied to you. I have smoked marijuana multiple times and I kept a small bag of it in the barn."

"Alright, thank you for clarifying that for me. Can you tell me how you acquired the weed?"

"Originally, it was a gift from a buddy of mine."

"Does your buddy have a name?" Moore asked plainly.

"Yes, but I'd rather not say who he is," James replied looking nervously at his father, who was frowning at him.

"Tell Detective Moore, who your friend is or else I'll disown you," Miller said emphatically.

Without further hesitation James blurted out, "His name is Eli Martin!"

"How long have you known Eli?" Moore asked patiently.

"About eight years. He was in my same grade in school and we belong to the same church. Eli and I are going through Rumspringa and that's how I've gotten to know him."

"Sounds to me like he hasn't been a very good influence on you," Moore commented. "Have either one of you ever sold drugs?"

"No, I don't think so. We both have apprenticeships with local farmers and craftsman and we earn a pretty good living considering our ages."

"What do you mean, 'I don't think so'?" Moore demanded. "You either did or did not sell drugs."

"I, uh mean, I haven't. And, I don't think Eli has; not that I know of, anyway."

"So, in other words, you never were dealers, only

buyers. Is that correct?"

"That's correct, Detective."

"Okay, let's move on. Recently James, I learned that your sister Rachael had THC in her system when she died. Were you aware that she smoked marijuana too?" Moore noticed beads of sweat forming on James' brow, when he inquired about Rachael's drug use.

James took of sip of water, stared at his father, and then responded meekly, "Yes."

"How long had she been smoking weed?" Moore asked coolly.

"For several months, I guess."

"Who gave her the marijuana?"

"I shared my stash with her," James said looking down at his hands and shaking his head.

"Do you want something to drink other than water, or do you want a short break before we proceed?" Moore asked politely.

"No, I'm fine for now," James replied, although beads of sweat continued forming on his forehead and he was wringing his hands.

"Alright, I'll proceed," Moore said.

"Who sold you the marijuana?"

James twisted in his seat apprehensively and said, "Honestly, I don't know her name, Detective."

"Come on James, you've been doing so well, thus far.

Please don't insult my intelligence. You know who she is," Moore said unapologetically.

"No, I don't, and neither does Eli. She showed up in a parking lot behind a convenience store where we were buying booze in a small town across the Ohio line in Indiana. She simply asked us if we wanted to buy some weed. We replied we did. She sold it to us and drove away."

"Did you ever buy from her again?"

"Yes, she told us she'd be at the same store the following week and she was."

"Where is the store located?"

"Woodburn, Indiana, but she switches around quite a bit. One time she would be in Indiana and then next time she would be in Ohio. Another time I met her in a gas station in Michigan."

"If I showed you a picture of her, do you think you could identify her?"

"I'm not certain. Eli and I switched paying for the stuff every other week or so. I don't know. Really, I was more concerned about looking out for the cops than I was remembering what she looked like." James remembered the warning the woman had given to him. *If you tell the authorities anything about me, I will hurt a member of your family.* He had not wanted to risk finding out if she was serious, and he still didn't. *I can't put another one of my family members in jeopardy!* He thought.

"What kind of vehicle did she drive?" Moore asked

pointedly.

"It was a plain, beige-colored, late model Chevrolet. It was starting to rust around the rear wheels and the paint on top of the car appeared to be fading. The interior was beige. Nothing fancy, just transportation."

"When you made your purchases, was there ever anyone else in the car with her?"

James thought for a moment, then shook his head and said, "No, she was always alone."

"Can you describe what she looked like?" Moore asked again. "Remember James, you promised to be completely truthful," Moore said looking directly into James' eyes.

James looked over at his father. Jacob looked back sternly at his son and nodded.

"Uh, okay, I'll try, Detective. Usually, she wore a grey-hooded, exercise top, and jeans. The hoodie was always tied, but she had brown hair. She was not real attractive. I'd guess she was in her mid to late twenties. Whenever we did business, she always was wearing dark sunglasses. She had kind of a southern or hillbilly accent, and she was a little chunky. She generally wore no lip stick or make-up. She looked plain and her skin color was lily-white, like she was never out in the sun. That's about all I can remember about her, Detective," James said imploringly.

"Why did you share your weed with your younger sister?"

"Well, uh, she asked me about what it felt like after I started smoking it. I guess you could say she was fairly

curious. I could tell she really wanted to try it, so I told her it wouldn't hurt her and it would make her feel happy and relaxed for an hour or so. Which it does!" James said with a touch of defiance in his voice.

"Did you have sex with Rachael when she tried smoking weed?" Moore asked matter-of-factly.

"I already told you, Detective, that I never had sex with Rachael!" James shot a glance at his father, who was shaking his head in disgust.

"Yes, and you also told me you never smoked marijuana before either," Moore said firing back at the young man.

James squirmed nervously in his chair and was beginning to sweat profusely. But after just a short pause, he met Moore's gaze and said, "We never were sexually involved. I admit we occasionally fooled around. I touched her and kissed her, but I never had actual sex with her."

"Did she try to block your advances, James?"

"She did at first, a little bit, but she eventually told me she enjoyed it. But after just a few times I came to my senses and stopped. I let her know we wouldn't be doing that sort of thing anymore." James shot another glance at his father, who just sat quietly shaking his head.

"James, do you really expect me to believe you stopped pursuing her for sexual favors. I was a horny, sixteen-year-old kid once in my life. My hormones were working 24/7 to have sex with someone, anyone. I was not particular."

"Well, Detective, I admit my hormones are sometimes

out of control, but apparently I was raised differently than you," James said proudly. He looked up into his father's eyes, and said emphatically, "I did not have sex with my sister." Jacob wore a look of disappointment on his weathered face and looked away from his son. James took hold of his father's hand and asked, "You believe me, don't you papa?"

"Boy, how could you have thought it was alright to fool around with your younger sister and kiss her? Frankly, I'm not sure what to believe," Jacob said staring into James' eyes.

Taking control of the interrogation again, Moore said, "Isn't it true James, that you gave Rachael the weed in hopes that it would induce her to have sex with you? And, isn't it true that when she gave in to your advances, you continued to give her pot so you could have sex with her?"

James started sobbing and in a broken voice admitted, "Okay, yes, I had sex with Rachael several times." His shoulders heaved and he turned away from his father.

"Okay," Moore said calmly. Now that he had broken James' will and his resistance to telling the full truth, Moore intended to find out whether James had anything to do with his sister's death. "Thanks for telling me the truth, James. I know it was hard for you." Moore paused briefly. He looked the broken, young man up and down. James was bent forward, his body heaving as he continued sobbing. The expression on the elder Miller's face was that of total devastation. Apparently, James had held back confessing the truth to his father, even after the "Come to Jesus talk". Moore felt sincere compassion for the father

sitting across the table who'd just heard his son admit to engaging in sexual relations with his sister. Moore imagined Miller must be wondering where he'd gone wrong as a parent. Moore handed James a tissue to dry his eyes and poured a fresh glass of water for him.

When he realized the Detective was not done with his son, the elder Miller said, "I've heard enough. I'll wait outside." As Jacob got up to leave the room, Moore noticed tears beginning to fall from his eyes onto his cheeks. Moore intuited that Jacob did not want to be in the room, when the final question had to be answered by his son.

After the door closed behind Jacob, Moore resumed the interrogation. "James, would you please, now, tell me truthfully what you were doing on Monday night, December 19, 1988 between the hours of 6:00 and 9:00 p.m."

James sniffled, and then replied, "I was outside taking a long walk."

"Now, I understand from Jonathan's testimony that at 9:00 p.m. you and Joshua came upstairs to go to bed. Is that correct?"

"Yes."

"When were you aware that Rachael was pregnant?"

"She told me a couple of days after she missed her period."

"What did you tell her when you heard the news?"

"I told her I thought the condom I used should have worked. She said crossly, 'Obviously, it didn't.'"

"When did you find out that she had miscarried your baby?"

"I didn't know until you told me about it during our first meeting."

"What were you doing on your long walk, the night of the murder?"

"Nothing much. I was just worried about Rachael being pregnant, so, I took a walk to think about things. What we would tell our parents, siblings, and such. That was the reason for the walk."

"When you met Rachael in the barn on that fateful Monday night to discuss the situation, did you try to convince her to have a self-induced abortion?"

"No, I didn't." James looked imploringly at Moore and then over at Chilcott. "I didn't even know she was in the barn that evening!"

"James, it is my opinion that you went out to the barn that evening to discuss options with her. Maybe one of your friends told you how to get rid of the baby. And maybe, at first, she decided to go along with you. But then, she changed her mind and objected. You became frustrated with her for backing out on the plan you made, so you shoved her. She accidentally fell against the spike and collapsed. Isn't that what happened James?" Moore stared at James while waiting for a response.

James' mouth worked, like he was trying to respond, but no words came out.

So, Moore pressed on, "Maybe you tried to help her,

but when you realized she was dead, you were scared and fled the barn. When you returned to the house, you felt so frightened and ashamed of yourself for putting Rachael through so much misery and pain, you didn't know what to do or who to turn to. First, there was the unplanned pregnancy. Then, a miscarriage. What was going through your mind?" Moore's voice rose as he demanded, "Why did you kill her, James? After causing so much heartbreak and pain for your sister, why did you want her dead?"

"I didn't want her dead!" James yelled angrily. "Look Detective, I've admitted to having sexual relations with Rachael and that I knew she had become pregnant. But I loved my sister, and I did not harm her in any way except that I got her knocked up. You can pressure me for hours and I'll tell you the same thing. I did nothing to harm her. I didn't push her, and I wasn't in the barn that evening. I'm guilty of having sex with her, but not of accidental murder or homicide."

"Are you sure about that?" Moore asked skeptically.

"Yes," James replied. "I realize having sex with your sister is a sin, forbidden by God's laws and by man's. But I would never have harmed Rachael. I loved her in spite of how I acted."

Moore couldn't be one-hundred percent sure, but he believed the young man was telling him the truth. The usual signs of deceit were not apparent when it counted, and his experience told him James was not responsible for Rachael's death. Moore instructed Chilcott to have James write a statement concerning the sexual activity between the two siblings and then he left the room.

Waiting inside the observation room were Sheriff Jackson and Samuel Murphy, the Grant County Prosecutor. When he entered the room, Murphy said, "I'd like to compliment you on your investigatory procedures. I presume you believe your suspect did not commit the murder?"

"Yes, frankly I'm surprised. His motive would have been to try to destroy the evidence of his sister's pregnancy and to cover up the fact that they were having sexual relations. I think we need to wait on the remaining evidence currently being processed, in order to determine who our next suspect will be. I assume Counselor that you will not be pursuing any charges for incest, given the current Ohio laws concerning that act. Am I correct?"

"Yes, you are correct, Detective Moore. As far as I'm concerned, you can release James Miller to his father, as soon as possible. I don't need to create any unnecessary friction between Grant County and the Amish community.

Sheriff Jackson strode over to Moore, patted his underling on the back, and said, "I thought once he confessed to the sexual relationship, it would be a slam dunk concerning the murder. But I agree with you. As far as I'm concerned, the young man didn't do it. Good job on the interrogation. You could have asked him to take a lie-detector test, but after listening to him, I don't think it's necessary."

"Thank you, gentlemen," Moore said. "I appreciate your confidence and trust in me. Once he's completed his statement, I'll have Chilcott release him to his father."

Chapter 17

The Ohio Bureau of Criminal Investigation (BCI) is located about a half-hour drive from the capitol city of Columbus, Ohio. The agency was founded on July 9, 1921 in London, Ohio. It began as a minor records keeping facility in conjunction with the Department of Public Welfare. Over the years, the BCI has seen many changes. During its early years, inmate labor from the London, Ohio prison facility performed most of the work. Archives reveal the inmates reviewed, indexed, and sorted fingerprint records. In 1963, the BCI was taken over by the Attorney General's Office and given a broader range of activities. It was reorganized into five separate divisions: identification, laboratory, investigations, administration, and data systems.

Moore sent the paper cup, the lid, and the plastic straw, found near the front of the Millers' barn to the Bureau of Criminal Investigation for analysis. The laboratory was usually able to process the information more quickly than the FBI. However, if the BCI couldn't find a match, Moore intended to forward the items to the FBI. The BCI records contained fingerprint index cards and DNA information for criminals that were caught and sent to jail in Ohio. Of course, in regards to the paper cup, the investigators were hoping to lift a latent print from the cup which could be compared in the BCI's data base. The straw would likely contain DNA evidence from saliva. Detective Moore was hoping for a hit on either one or both of the items sent for analysis.

Two weeks after they'd interrogated James Miller and released him, Moore received a facsimile from the BMI. The facsimile report indicated there was a positive match on both the fingerprint and the DNA sample obtained from the paper cup and the plastic straw. Moore was ecstatic, when he saw the possible suspect was a local resident and an ex-con. The man lived somewhere in Wayne. *Finally, I've got a solid lead,* he thought.

The ex-con's name was Charles L. Holland. Holland was thirty-years-old, a one-time offender, and had been convicted of burglary ten years earlier. He had served five years at the corrections facility in Orient, Ohio. The prison was fifteen miles away from Columbus. Originally, Holland's family moved from eastern Kentucky to northern Ohio to seek employment in the auto industry. Chilcott checked out Holland's record and conferred with his former parole officer. Chilcott reported to Moore that Holland had a clean record after getting paroled.

On Friday morning, Moore assigned Chilcott to find out Holland's current address, place of employment, and whether he owned a motor vehicle or not. Moore also wanted to know if Holland had had any recent minor scrapes with law enforcement officials, which were not reported.

After reviewing the records, Chilcott reported to Moore that Holland lived on the south side of Wayne, right off Main St. on 3rd St. Holland had managed to avoid any scrapes with the law after being released from prison. He drove a 1984 Chevrolet pick-up truck. Holland was employed by a family-owned company in Wayne, called Swanson Seating. Swanson Seating manufactured specialty seating for the front seats of buses and motor homes. He'd worked his way up to the final-finish department. Holland had been employed with Swanson ever since he'd gotten out of prison.

Around 6:00 p.m. Moore and Chilcott drove by his 3rd St. home. There were no lights on and the officers wondered if he was at home. They rang the doorbell several times, but there was no answer. The home was quiet and appeared unoccupied.

The following morning, Chilcott called Swanson Seating and asked to speak to Holland. Chilcott was told he worked the second shift. Around noon, Moore and Chilcott knocked on his front door again. Holland came to the door in a robe. He was short, red-haired, and two of his lower rear teeth were missing. Moore flashed his badge and Holland invited the officers in without hesitation.

Holland gestured toward a couch in the living room. Moore took a seat, but Chilcott remained standing. Holland politely asked, "What can I do for you officers?"

Meanwhile, Chilcott was accessing Holland's home. He wandered around the living room making note of the well-worn condition of the furniture. Otherwise, the interior of the rental house appeared to be clean and neat for a bachelor pad

Moore said, "We'd like to ask you several questions."

"Okay," Holland responded.

"Mr. Holland," Moore said plainly, "Can you tell me what you were doing on the night of Monday, December 19, 1988?"

"I don't remember, but I was probably at work. I work the second shift," Holland replied unperturbed.

"What if I told you on that Monday evening, you'd taken the day off?"

"It's possible. I could check my calendar," he said appearing to be puzzled. *What do these cops want from me? I haven't done anything wrong.*

"That won't be necessary, your employer confirmed you were off that day," Moore said.

"Hey, what's this about?" Holland was now clearly agitated.

"Why do you think we're here, Charles?"

"I don't have a clue," Holland responded honestly.

"On December 19, 1988, did you go anywhere in the evening?"

"I really don't remember. Oh, wait a minute; I met a woman at a Hamilton Lake restaurant for dinner."

"Where is Hamilton Lake?" Moore asked.

"It's right across the border in Hamilton, Indiana. It's about an hour's drive from here."

"Who was the woman?"

"Someone, I'd previously met who lives on Hamilton Lake."

"Does she have a name?"

"Yes, her name is Datha Williams." Holland replied, but then demanded, "So what's this about anyway?"

"Just answer the questions, please, Mr. Holland. We'll get to what my inquiry is about in a few minutes," Moore replied flatly. "Now, what time did you meet Datha Williams?"

"Well, I was supposed to meet her at 5:00 p.m., but a deer ran out in front of my truck. I ended up in a ditch and my right front fender was damaged. I had to get a farmer to pull me out. If you don't believe me go look at my truck. I haven't had the money to fix it yet," Holland said unhappily.

Moore smiled and said, "I'll do that right now." He motioned to Chilcott to continue with the interrogation as he rose from the couch and walked outside to examine Holland's truck.

"What time did you finally arrive in Hamilton, Charles?" Chilcott asked.

"I was an hour late."

"What time did you return home after having dinner with Ms. Williams?"

"The following morning around 10:00 a.m. We spent the night together at her cottage after dinner."

"When you ended up in the ditch, did you know where you were?"

"Sort of, I was on County Road W200S, about nine or ten miles outside of Wayne."

"Did you get the name of the farmer, who pulled you out of the ditch?"

"No, I didn't. But I could take you to his farm house, if I need to," Holland replied.

"I don't know if that will be necessary or not," Chilcott stated. "But I'll keep your offer in mind."

After returning from inspecting the pick-up truck, Moore had been standing in the entrance to the living room listening to Chilcott questioning Holland. He interjected, "Thanks for your time and trouble Mr. Holland. Have a nice day. You aren't planning on leaving town in the next couple of days, are you?"

"No, I'm not planning on going anywhere. I've got to work," Holland said as he stood and opened the front door for the officers to leave. "But you didn't tell me why I'm being interrogated," Holland said peevishly.

Moore smiled and nodded his head as he passed Holland. As he walked toward the police car, he said over his shoulder, "We'll be in touch, Mr. Holland."

When Moore got into the police car, Chilcott immediately asked, "Is the pick-up damaged, like Holland said?"

"Yup, it is. He was truthful about that."

Next, Chilcott asked excitedly, "How did I do, you know, with my line of questions?"

"I thought you did fine, Randy. You'll make a fine detective someday when I'm done training you." Moore patted Chilcott on the shoulder. "Holland seemed pretty calm, until I asked him what he was doing the night of December 19, 1988."

"Yes, and then he started getting agitated and seemed rather nervous. I think we better check out his alibi before we come to any conclusion," Chilcott said.

"That's the right conclusion to draw, Randy. We may have to have Holland show us where that farmer lives. His claim that the farmer pulled him out of the ditch shouldn't be too hard to verify. And, if his alibi is confirmed, I guess we'll have to drop him as a suspect. You can't be in two places at the same time, Sergeant." *I think Randy is finally starting to make the kind of progress I'd like to see. And, it's about damn time.*

"Yes, I know you're right, Captain," Chilcott replied.

"Let's go out to County Road W200S and see if we can see where he claims his truck ran off the road. The farm can't be too far from there."

"It seems to me like he passed the Miller farm and was several miles down the road where he ended up in the ditch," Chilcott said.

"If we can find where the accident occurred, we might get lucky and find the farmhouse where the farmer lives.

And, if the farmer is at home, we can easily verify Holland's alibi."

Several miles past the Miller farm, Chilcott spotted what looked like a tire mark on the side of the road that indicated someone had gone off into the drainage ditch below. The ground in the ditch was damaged and torn up. A farm house sat right across the road where the accident occurred. They pulled into the driveway and a tall man quickly appeared. He was at least six-foot five-inches tall, with a large belly and a broad smile. Chilcott put down the window, showed him his badge, and asked, "By any chance did you pull a red Chevrolet pick-up truck out of that ditch approximately two weeks ago?" Chilcott pointed at the ditch across the road.

"Yes sir, I did," the farmer responded genially.

"Do you remember about what time it was when you pulled him out?" Chilcott asked.

"Yes, I do. My wife always has supper on the table at 5:00 p.m. sharp and I was just sitting down to eat dinner, when I heard a knock on the front door. A man, maybe thirtyish, appeared at my front door and asked if I could pull him out of the ditch. He told me a deer jumped out in front of him and caused him to run off the road. So, I helped him."

"That was nice of you," Chilcott said with a touch of disappointment.

"Yes, the driver gave me a twenty-dollar bill and said he was in a hurry. He was late for a date."

Moore pulled out a mug shot of Holland from his

pocket and showed it to the farmer. “Was this the man?” Moore asked.

“Yes, that’s him. But he looked a bit older to me in person.”

“Thank you for your time and trouble, sir,” Moore replied.

Chilcott started the car, pulled out of the driveway, and headed back to Wayne.

“Well, we’ll check with Ms. Williams to confirm Holland got there at 6:00 p.m. and spent the night with her. Assuming she confirms his alibi, I guess we’ll have to look for another suspect. *There has got to be something else,* Moore thought. *What am I missing? I’ll need more leads in order to solve this case.*

Chapter 18

Moore sent the tire impression to the FBI for analysis on December 22, 1988. The impression was molded from the tread marks still visible in the frozen dirt on the access road. The access road was between the corn field and the barn and the marks were found about fifty-feet from the entrance to the county road.

By mid-January, 1989 Moore had still not heard back from the FBI's office in Columbus. He assumed the tire-impression mold was sent on to the FBI crime lab in Quantico, Virginia for processing. Moore was hopeful the lab techs would be able to identify the size and type of tire. Then, he'd have a good chance of determining the vehicle make and model that used that particular tire size and style. He'd already taken a photograph of the tread marks to a local tire store to see if the manager could help identify it. But he had no idea and was no help.

Detective Moore expected the results of the tire impression examination to arrive in the next week or so from the FBI. In the meantime, he wondered how the BCI was coming on identifying the latent print found on the window pane outside the barn. His team carefully removed the pane and sent it to the FBI at the same time the tire impression was sent. He expected to get the fingerprint results from the flashlight back from the BCI before getting the results from the FBI.

The investigators found several latent fingerprints on the flashlight. The BCI had already identified Rachael's right index fingerprint taken from the underside of the flashlight opposite from the light switch. The other fingerprints did not match anyone in the Miller household. And, the BCI couldn't find a match to it in their data base either. The BCI decided to send the flashlight to the FBI for further analysis and so notified Detective Moore. He was awaiting that report as well.

In the meantime, Chilcott contacted Ms. Datha Williams in Hamilton, Indiana. She verified Holland's story and reluctantly admitted they had spent the night together on December 19, 1988. Chilcott told Moore that she seemed embarrassed to admit that Holland had spent the night at her home.

Moore thought sarcastically, *Gee I wonder why? After all, they were not married and this was a first date.* Sometimes he questioned Chilcott's thought process. Ms. Williams was known to be a respected member of the community and active member of her church. *Of course, she was embarrassed and concerned about her good reputation in the community.*

Chilcott had compiled a thorough background investigation of Datha Williams that established her as a credible witness. Moore also questioned Chilcott's understanding of societal norms, but decided that he offered more pluses than minuses. He wondered when Chilcott first met Monica. *Had Randy overlooked her licentious character in favor of her loose sexual behavior?*

Late Friday afternoon, Moore received a facsimile from the FBI about the unknown prints found on the flashlight. The information indicated that they belonged to Randy Chilcott, who resided in Wayne, Ohio. Moore was flabbergasted. *How could that be? I saw him put on gloves prior to picking up the flashlight.*

Moore walked down the hall to Chilcott's glass cubical office and pronounced in an unusually loud voice, which blared over the glass partition, "Randy, if you've got a minute, I'd like to talk to you in my office."

Chilcott eyed his boss warily. He could see that Moore was agitated. "Sure, I'll be right there, Captain," he answered. Within fifteen seconds, Chilcott stood in front of Moore's desk. "What can I do for you, Boss?"

"There's been a development in the Miller case you need to explain!" Moore was fuming. Chilcott stared blankly back at Moore awaiting the news. Moore demanded, "How the hell did your fingerprints get on that flashlight?"

"I guess you caught me," Chilcott replied with a sheepish grin. "I screwed up and touched the flashlight before putting on my gloves. As soon as I caught myself picking the light up, I realized I'd made a mistake and dropped the flashlight on the straw covered floor. I probably should have said something at the time, but I was too embarrassed to tell you. Besides, I wasn't sure I'd left a fingerprint impression anyway. I held the flashlight very loosely. Captain, I was trying to make a good impression on you and I knew screwing up wasn't going to get me anywhere. I should have said something, but I didn't. I'm sorry I messed up." Chilcott looked humiliated. His already, overly red face turned scarlet.

"What was I doing that I didn't catch your error?" Moore asked angrily.

"I think you were looking out the window at the falling snow."

Moore grunted, and replied, "Well, I guess it's no big deal, Randy. People make mistakes all the time. That's what keeps us employed, right?" He frowned, then added, "Please, in the future try to be more careful. This kind of thing is embarrassing."

"Thanks, Boss. I hoped you wouldn't be too mad at me for making the mistake." Chilcott sounded genuinely sorry. "I'll do better for sure in the future."

"Alright, I'm not going to chew you out any more. Just go back to work."

"Yes sir! I will." Chilcott's face was starting to change back to its normal shade.

I'll bet he almost crapped his underwear when he realized I caught his mistake. He looked and acted embarrassed and ashamed. Sorry about that, but bad things happen when you forget procedures and make a mistake.

Detective Moore thought that Randy Chilcott was

basically a capable law enforcement officer, but under pressure he could be forgetful. Case in point, forgetting to put on his rubber gloves before processing important evidentiary items.

On his way out the door, Moore asked Chilcott if he had any plans for the weekend. Chilcott indicated he did not. So, Moore invited him to come out on Saturday around noon for a cookout. He felt sorry for his partner, knowing he was probably going to be alone. Chilcott accepted the invitation and was pleased that Moore seemed to have forgiven him for the error so quickly. But Moore did not forget his underling's failure to follow procedure, even though he decided to let it slide for the time being.

"Can I bring something?" Chilcott hoped this would be an opportunity to mend fences with his boss.

Moore appreciated the gesture, and replied, "Why don't you bring a twelve-pack of beer. Jean likes to drink Bud Light."

"Bud Light it is, Boss. I'll be there a little before noon," Chilcott promised.

"Do you like to ice fish, Randy?"

"Not really, Captain," Chilcott said regrettably.

"Too bad. Lately, I've been catching large crappies and blue gills by the dozens. Hancock Lake was restocked a few years ago and there aren't many fishermen because it's a privately owned lake."

"Really? I didn't know that. I thought Hancock was publicly owned." Chilcott was now beaming with confidence that Moore had seemingly lost any interest in how and why Chilcott's finger print was on the flashlight.

"If you paid my property taxes, you'd realize it," Moore said jokingly. "I've got to run. Jean is waiting for me to take her out to dinner. I don't want to be late. See you tomorrow."

"See you tomorrow, Boss," Chilcott said smiling.

"Don't forget to bring the beer," Moore said as he pulled on his coat and walked toward the exit from the Detective Bureau.

During his drive home Moore wondered about something. He was aware that whenever a law enforcement officer was hired, their prints and background information are sent to the FBI for a routine criminal search. And, before officially becoming a sworn officer, that search must not show any criminal activity in the past. This was standard procedure for all law enforcement agencies. He also knew the FBI rarely retained those non-criminal prints and, if they did, they were not readily accessible or searchable. So, he wondered why Randy's prints were still available and in existence in the FBI database. He made a mental note that on Monday morning he would make an inquiry.

* * *

First thing Monday morning, he contacted the FBI and requested an explanation as to why Chilcott's fingerprints were still in their database. The charge officer, who responded, said, "I have no idea." So, one of their people must have made a mistake. *Well, if the FBI isn't worried, why should I be?* The explanation satisfied Moore's curiosity.

* * *

Near the end of January, 1989, the Federal Bureau of Investigation finally issued its report on the tire impression. The report stated that the tire's size was P195/75R14 and that the tire was an all-weather tire. Unfortunately, that size tire was manufactured by several different companies. It was a popular size and used on over twenty different models of vehicles. There was not much Moore could learn from the tire tread impression mold taken from the Miller farm. He was disappointed with the report.

However, Moore was pleased to learn that a Monica Slidell of Wheeling, West Virginia had apparently left her right index fingerprint on the Millers' barn window pane. To Moore's amazement, after a brief investigation he learned that Monica Slidell was none other than Chilcott's former girlfriend, Monica Kerlin. Kerlin apparently married a Billy Slidell in West Virginia and divorced him a year later in 1984. Monica did not have an extensive criminal record, but she was arrested in late 1984 for prostitution and burglary. She served a nine-month stint in the Ohio County Jail located in Wheeling, West Virginia.

The report also stated that she was born and raised in Morgantown, West Virginia. *Maybe she migrated north to Grant County, Ohio to get a new start. But why was her print at the crime scene?* Her record did not alert Moore to any violent behavior in her past. He wondered how much Randy knew about Monica's past. He assumed not much; although they had been living together for the past two years.

After deliberating about whether to inform Chilcott about his former girlfriend's finger print on the window pane, Moore decided that she would have to be considered a suspect or, at least, a person of interest. After all, her latent print was found at the crime scene. Reluctantly, he decided to share the news with his subordinate.

Upon hearing the news about his former sweetheart, Monica Kerlin or Monica Slidell, Chilcott seemed shocked. He expressed relief that she was out of his life.

"Randy, I know this will be difficult for you, but do you think you can help find Monica?" Moore asked Chilcott. "We need to find out what she was doing at the Miller farm and why her print was on the window pane."

"Well Boss, frankly, uh… Monica never really talked much about her past. I always believed she was keeping something from me. But I assumed she was embarrassed to talk about it. I think she's had a pretty hard life."

"Did you ever imagine she might be capable of murder?" Moore gently inquired.

"Not really, but in this business, I've seen all kinds of people commit crimes," Chilcott replied.

"Unfortunately, you're right," Moore agreed. "You told me she said she was going to stay with her mother. Is that correct?"

"Yes, that's what she told me."

"Did she tell you where her mother lives?"

"She once mentioned Charleston, West Virginia. But I got the impression her mom moved around a lot. The name Monica used for her mother is Dorothy Kerlin, but who knows for sure. That could be her maiden name, but she might have been married before."

"Did Monica ever talk about her father?"

"She mentioned once that they'd never met. I don't know if Dorothy ever married him or took his name. Some of the Appalachia people have, shall we say, varied pasts. Many are moonshiners, others deal in illegal drugs, and some steal automobiles. They are born and raised tough and often times survive on very little."

"Yes, I've had some involvement with their kind in my past law enforcement career in Chicago," Moore interjected. "I'm sure if they want to go off the grid, they can."

"So, how do you want me to proceed?" Chilcott asked expectantly.

"First, let's look for her in Charleston, West Virginia. Let's see if you can develop any leads there."

"Okay Boss," Chilcott replied without hesitation.

"Oh, by the way, do you have any photographs of

Monica we could send to other police agencies to help us locate her?"

"Sure, I've got one or two, unless she took them with her when she left."

"Well, if she is guilty of homicide, she might have taken the photos with her to cover her tracks. We do have a mug shot of her in any case. She might look a few years younger, but so what. Of course, it's not hard for a woman to change the way she looks, if she has a reason to change her appearance. Women can change the color of their hair, apply different types of make-up, either gain or lose weight, get a tan, wear glasses, and look quite differently by what they wear."

"I'll see if I can get a recent photo, Captain."

* * *

The following day, Chilcott appeared in Moore's office. "I found a recent picture of Monica and myself at the Sheriff's Picnic last summer. I instructed the photography people at CVS to blow her picture up and crop me out. No need to see my face. I'm not a suspect in a homicide," Chilcott said with an amused chuckle. "CVS printed a 5 X 7 photo of her for us to use and it's even in color. What do you think, Boss?" Chilcott was practically beaming as he handed the photo to Moore.

As Moore gazed at the picture, he said, "Looks pretty good to me. How are you coming on locating Monica or her mother, Randy?"

"Not very well, it seems," Chilcott said. "It's as if she was intending to disappear. You know, thinking back on the events that preceded her departure, I wonder if she had planned to do it like this all along. Maybe you are right. She is a suspect. I hate to admit it, but I suppose she could be a killer."

"I know what you're going through, Randy. It's very hard and I'm sorry for you. But let's see how this plays out before we rush to any more premature judgments. Try to keep a stiff upper lip and be patient." Moore thought about how terrible it would be to discover that your girlfriend, wife, or lover might be a dangerous criminal. *I hope we can quickly find Monica and prove she was not responsible for Rachael's demise, for Chilcott's piece of mind.*

Chapter 19

After evidence emerged that Monica Kerlin's print was found outside on the Miller's barn window pane, Moore was concerned. And, after her sudden and unexpected departure from Chilcott's home, Moore realized she was a suspect. So, Moore prepared an all-points bulletin (APB) for Monica Kerlin aka Monica Slidell. He instructed Chilcott to send facsimiles of the APB along with her picture to the various state-wide and federal law enforcement agencies. Included in the APB was a brief explanation of why the authorities wanted to talk to her. The APB indicated that she was considered a person of interest in a homicide investigation. It also indicated that she was suspected of being a drug dealer.

That afternoon Moore instructed Chilcott to go to the Jacob Miller farm and show Monica's picture to Miller's son, James. He hoped James would be able to identify her as the person he'd purchased marijuana from on several occasions. Moore also told him to contact Eli Martin, James Miller's friend and former classmate. Hopefully, he'd be able to identify her as well.

For the moment, the investigation seemed to be

proceeding rather nicely, Moore thought. But he knew that there were always going to be things that could unexpectedly change the investigation's course. Moore believed, Monica Kerlin might be more than a person of interest and maybe she was a killer. The question was: What was her motive?

Although Chilcott had previously been cleared of having any criminal past by the FBI, Moore was mildly concerned about Randy Chilcott. He hoped Chilcott's relationship with Monica had never gotten in the way of his good judgment. So, Moore obtained Chilcott's personnel file with the permission of Sheriff Roger Jackson and began to look into Chilcott's past.

He told Sheriff Jackson that out of an abundance of caution, he needed to make sure Sergeant Chilcott was not involved with his girlfriend in any criminal activity. Jackson agreed and said it would be a huge embarrassment to the Grant County Sheriff's Department if one of their officers was involved in any wrong doing. Moore indicated there was no evidence to suspect that Chilcott was involved. But Moore realized that blind love can sometimes change a person's good character and alter their normally good judgment. Jackson approved of Moore's request to review Chilcott's personnel file and instructed his office clerk, Nellie Price, to give the file to Captain Moore. The Sheriff also instructed Price to not discuss the matter at all. He never gave her an explanation as to why Moore needed the file. Price complied with his request and thought maybe Randy was up for a promotion.

Moore understood that personnel files could only offer

a glimpse of the past. If you really want to find out about a person's past, you have to talk to former friends, neighbors, ex-girlfriends, employers, and law enforcement officials in the community where the person grew up and lived.

Chilcott's personnel file indicated that he'd grown up on a farm in Akron, Indiana. Akron is about forty miles do west of Fort Wayne, Indiana. It is located at the juncture of Indiana 19 and 114. The road map indicated it was out in the middle of nowhere in farm country. Moore would have liked to do his research over the telephone, but he didn't know who in the area to talk too. So, Moore asked Jackson to approve a two-day visit to Akron. After receiving Jackson's approval Moore booked a motel room for one night just outside of Fort Wayne. Moore realized investigating a subordinate wasn't particularly unusual for someone of his rank. But Grant County didn't have any internal investigation staff to utilize. In lieu of asking for assistance from the Ohio State Highway Patrol, Sheriff Jackson and Captain Moore were going to oversee their own internal investigation of Chilcott unbeknownst to the rest of the Sheriff's Department staff.

Day one, Moore wanted to visit where Chilcott had grown up. He was amazed at how flat the terrain was as he made the half-hour drive from his motel room to Chilcott's boyhood home just outside of Akron. When he arrived at the address, it was apparent the farm house was abandoned. However, the land had been tilled and the remnants of a corn crop was still visible in the field. Moore assumed another farmer had purchased the land and had cultivated and harvested a substantial corn crop the past year. The barren fields spanned quite a distance. Moore noticed a farm house down the road.

Moore stopped at the farm house and was greeted by an aging farmer, who looked to be in his early seventies. He got out of his cruiser and said hello. The farmer seemed cautious at first, but after several minutes of conversation, he warmed to the detective. Moore showed the farmer his shield and indicated he was with the Grant County Sheriff's Department in Ohio. He said his mission was to learn about Randy Chilcott. The farmer indicated that he had known Chilcott and his family, but hadn't seen Randy for five years. Moore stipulated to the farmer that Chilcott wasn't in any trouble and was being considered for a position on the Sheriff's Department. Moore explained that he was there to check on Chilcott's character and verify background information according to departmental procedures.

The farmer, Larry Neff, attested to Chilcott's good character and indicated the family had been neighbors of his for many years. Neff said that after Chilcott's father passed his mother sold the farm and moved to Wabash to live with Chilcott's younger sister, Teresa. He hadn't seen either the mother or the daughter in several years. Neff told Moore the Chilcott's were simple people, who raised their crops, attended church, and kept to themselves. He never heard anything bad about Randy or any of the other family members. Moore was satisfied and thanked the farmer for his help. Following the conversation with Neff, Moore headed into the small retail area of Akron.

After driving around Akron, Moore's next stop was

Rochester, Indiana, the county seat of Fulton County, Indiana. The small berg of Akron was located in Fulton County and Moore planned to talk to the Sheriff and see if he knew the Chilcott family, and in particular, Randy Chilcott. When he arrived at the Sheriff's Department he was impressed with the facility. There was a tall chain-link fence that surrounded the multiple-building complex. He thought it looked like it had been recently constructed. He parked his unmarked cruiser in a visitor parking space near the front of the building. Moore exited his dark blue Ford Crown Victoria cruiser and went inside. He identified himself to the officer at the information window, showed his Detective's shield, and asked to speak to the Sheriff.

After waiting ten minutes, a tall and very thin Deputy Sheriff greeted him and took him to Sheriff John Nelson's first floor office. Moore was impressed with the newness of the facility. There were nicely painted walls, brand new office equipment, large windows, and an abundance of modern police equipment. Sheriff Nelson greeted Moore when he entered the office. Out of professional courtesy Moore displayed his Detective's shield to Nelson. Nelson instructed him to have a seat. Moore compiled. Nelson relayed the message to Moore that Sheriff Roger Jackson had called and explained his captain's visit. Nelson assured Moore that his department would cooperate fully with the inquiry. Moore wasn't surprised that Sheriff Jackson called to give Sheriff Nelson a heads up on his visit. He wondered if Jackson had met Nelson personally at the National Sheriff's Association meetings over the years.

Sheriff Nelson admitted to knowing the Chilcott family. "It's a fairly small county and I've gotten to know a lot of people during my career as a law enforcement officer," Nelson stated. "The Chilcott's were staunch supporters of the Farm Bureau," he explained. "Chilcott's father had been a long-standing member of the Fulton County Sheriff's auxiliary association too," Nelson added.

Moore inquired whether the son, Randy Chilcott, had ever gotten into trouble or engaged in any criminal behavior. Nelson responded, "I never saw or heard his name mentioned in any criminal investigation in Fulton County. Randy was a good student, played sports, and didn't hang around with the wrong crowd. As far as I know, Randy Chilcott was an honest and honorable young man. I'd be surprised if Chilcott had significantly changed much over the years."

Moore thanked him and decided to end this phase of the investigation into Chilcott's past. He was convinced Sergeant Randy Chilcott wouldn't have been involved in any crime. The evidence indicated that Randy was a man of excellent character.

Moore spent an hour that night writing a report to be given to Sheriff Jackson the following morning. The next day, he got up very early, intending to be back in the office by 7:30 a.m. Prior to leaving the motel, Moore called his wife, Jean, and told her he would be returning home that day.

Chapter 20

After returning from his trip to Akron, Indiana, Moore met with Sheriff Jackson and submitted a report about his visit to Randy Chilcott's home town. They both agreed there was no pressing need to pursue any further activity concerning the character of Sergeant Chilcott, at least for the time being. But they definitely wanted to learn more about Monica Kerlin.

Chilcott informed Moore later in the day that both Eli Martin and James Miller identified Monica Kerlin as the person from whom they'd purchased drugs. Moore informed Sheriff Jackson about Kerlin's drug sales activity involving two separate Amish youths. Moore realized this created a serious problem. Sheriff Jackson made the difficult decision to search Randy Chilcott's home, even though Kerlin was no longer residing there. Monica spent two years living with Randy, so Jackson reasoned there could be criminal evidence in Chilcott's home that she'd left behind. Moore agreed.

Jackson quickly contacted a judge and supplied him with the evidence already in existence against Kerlin. A search warrant was issued. Chilcott was naturally anxious about his home being searched but understood the necessity. He agreed to the search and was there to open the house up for the officers. Sergeant Chilcott was not invited to participate in the search of his property. Jackson was relieved to learn that Chilcott approved of the search.

Moore and Sheriff Jackson instructed the two officers on how to proceed with the search of Chilcott's home. They would assist with searching through Kerlin's remaining belongings left inside the house. It was understood by the officers that Chilcott's home would not be torn apart during the search.

Chilcott hoped the officers would adhere to that commitment. He was skeptical, but he decided to wait and see. He told Moore that he understood the reason for the search and was ashamed that Monica had put him into a very embarrassing and difficult position. Moore assured Chilcott that it wouldn't be a problem for him in the long run.

Randy Chilcott's home was on a large lot at the end of a quiet, dead-end street. To the left side of the house was a large woods and behind the home a plowed field. Chilcott lived in a ranch style, L-shaped house with a two-car garage. He had owned the home for the past five years. Monica Kerlin moved in with him in 1986. The home had light brown aluminum siding and the trim was painted white. The 1,500 square foot home was in good repair, although the lack of landscaping was not sufficient for the house. But there were nice shade trees in the yard. The house at one time had been a 1,250 sq. foot home with two bedrooms and one bath. However, a prior owner added a

250 sq. foot master bedroom suite before Chilcott purchased the home.

The search began inside Chilcott's two-car garage. When the officers went into the garage, they found Chilcott's unmarked police vehicle parked in one space. They also found another vehicle covered with a dark-colored cloth tarp parked in the other space. When they removed the tarp, they saw a 1983 Oldsmobile 2-door Cutlass Supreme, purple pearl-colored, with partially rusted-out rear fenders above the wheels. The on-duty Deputy checked the registration and learned the vehicle was registered to Randy Chilcott. Moore already knew about the vehicle and its owner. They inspected the vehicle further and Moore noted the tire size was a match to the tire impression that was made at the Miller farm the day after Rachael Miller's body was found. Moore instructed the officers to have the car impounded and towed to the Sheriff's Department garage for further examination.

As the wrecker service employee loaded up the Oldsmobile on a flatbed truck Chilcott was concerned, but he was not in a state of panic. He remembered leaving the hand gun tucked under the seat. He had forgotten to get rid of it. *Shit,* he thought, *I can't believe I left it there*. However, he doubted if the officers in the garage would do much more than compare the tire tread with the mold and maybe take some fingerprints. He'd been sure to wipe down and remove his prints from the vehicle. And, he wore gloves when he drove the car to Tennessee and back. Everything is going to be fine, he assured himself.

Meanwhile, Detective Moore remembered the

testimony of James Miller, who indicated Kerlin drove a late-model Chevrolet in poor repair. He thought, *there is not much difference between a Chevrolet and an Oldsmobile. The Amish boy could have mistaken the Oldsmobile for a Chevrolet; probably an honest mistake.* But he would photograph the vehicle and ask James Miller and Eli Martin to identify it. That James had originally described the vehicle as a Chevrolet could be used against the prosecution at a trial, so Moore wanted to clarify the record that the young men identified the vehicle from the photograph.

Moore noticed a square opening with a lid in the ceiling of the garage. He secured a ladder, climbed up to the lid, and discovered it was an access panel into the garage attic. He lifted the lid, placed it off to the side inside the attic, and looked around. The garage was heavily insulated with a blown-in cellulose insulation product that was approximately ten inches thick. Several feet from the opening he noticed an area that looked like it had been disturbed. Under the insulation, Moore found a large amount of marijuana in two cellophane bags placed inside a paper grocery sack. There were several bricks of marijuana and he estimated each brick to weigh approximately 2.2 pounds. Moore knew that type of marijuana was usually of poor quality and included stems, seeds, and leaves. Still, the street value would be several thousand dollars. Broken down and sold in dime bags, as the buyers and dealers called them, the marijuana could be sold for a lot more money than it was worth in bulk.

Sheriff Jackson and one of his deputies began searching the living room. Nothing of interest was found there. When

Moore completed his search of the garage, he and another officer started looking through the bedrooms. After searching the master bedroom around the bed and in the dresser drawers, nothing of interest was found other than a woman's clothing mixed in with a man's. The large dresser was half-full of women's clothing. Moore recalled that Chilcott had told him that Monica left the car and most of her clothing in the house when she left. Everything was consistent with Chilcott's story. There was no evidence to suggest Chilcott wasn't telling the truth.

Following the completion of an extensive search inside the kitchen, which turned up nothing of a criminal nature, both Moore and Sheriff Jackson proceeded to the basement. To their surprise they discovered that Chilcott had constructed an in-door shooting range, which they assumed he used during the winter months to occupy his time. The range allowed for firing small caliber weapons up to 50 feet on one side of the basement. The hot water heater, furnace, water softener, and a washer and dryer occupied the other side of the basement.

Chilcott had taken three, 4 x 4 sections of ¾ inch laminated plywood and placed a thick woven piece of carpeting between each plywood section. The sections were bolted together and the target was hung from ceiling joists by two large hooks. There were several paper targets on the large board. The hanging target contained many bullet holes. From the size of the holes, Moore assumed Randy had been shooting 22 caliber bullets on the range. Behind the hanging target, Chilcott had placed a 4 x 4 piece of quarter inch harden steel and hung it from the rafters to stop any bullet from ricocheting off his concrete wall. There was no insulation to deaden the noise inside the room, but two basement windows could be opened slightly to provide for better ventilation and to get rid of some of the sound.

Sheriff Jackson commented that no permit was required to have a home shooting range, although there was a noise ordinance. But who was going to complain about a local police officer who might occasionally shoot in his basement firing range? Besides, even if his neighbors could hear the noise, they might not be able to pin-point the location of the sounds. Chilcott's neighborhood consisted mostly of singles and young families. The older residents chose to live in other parts of the city.

In addition to the shooting range, Chilcott had constructed a partitioned wall with a ¾ inch piece of plywood. The wall had an opening to shoot through as an added safety feature. There was a small table and chair in the room. Above the table, a 22-caliber weapon was stored in a locked metal cabinet mounted on the wall. Inside the cabinet was Chilcott's registered 22-caliber Smith and Wesson handgun, some ammunition, ear plugs, and safety glasses. When Chilcott unlocked the cabinet, Moore noted the handgun had a trigger locking device and was enclosed in a plastic traveling case. It was the only gun found inside the home other than his 9-millimeter Glock 19 police-issued handgun, which was found locked away in his bedroom and secured in a small safe mounted in the closet. Everything concerning the storage and placement of the firearms and ammunition was in order.

There was a small out-building used to store a snow

blower, lawnmower, leaf blower, and some garden tools behind his house. The building was searched and nothing out of the ordinary was found. Sheriff Jackson, Captain Moore, and the two assisting officers completed the search of Chilcott's home in less than four hours. They'd found Monica's clothing, a substantial amount of weed, and thought they'd found the car described by James Miller. Nothing else of an incriminating nature was found in the home.

* * *

Sheriff Jackson made another difficult decision the following Monday morning, January 30, 1989. He decided to suspend Sergeant Randy Chilcott from duty without pay until the investigation of Monica Kerlin was completed. Of course, Chilcott didn't take the news very well. He was told by Sheriff Jackson to turn in his badge and his sidearm to Captain Moore. Since Chilcott didn't own another vehicle other than the one that Monica drove, he had to rent another vehicle, until his car was returned from the Sheriff's department garage. He'd handed the keys to his police car to Moore on his way out of the Sheriff's Department door.

Moore felt kind of sorry for Chilcott for getting entangled in a messy police investigation of his former girlfriend and lover, Monica Kerlin. He realized Chilcott was not entirely at fault, but Chilcott's association with a troubled woman from West Virginia with a sketchy past was problematic. Moore shook Randy's hand and patted him on the back as Chilcott prepared to leave the office. Moore assured Chilcott as soon as the investigation was concluded, he would be reinstated and things would quickly go back to normal. Chilcott seemed to be appeased by his words.

Following Chilcott's departure, Moore faced the task of searching for Monica Kerlin, aka Monica Slidell, and her mother, Dorothy Kerlin, who supposedly was living in Charleston, West Virginia, according to Chilcott. Prior to his departure from the Sheriff's Department, Chilcott had given Moore his file on the on-going investigation and the whereabouts of the Kerlin women. Moore was anxious to get going on that segment of the investigation. With Chilcott out of the picture, he enlisted Deputy Sheriff Howard Lechlitner, on a part-time basis to help him. Moore had the unpleasant task of informing Deputy Lechlitner about Sergeant Chilcott's suspension. Lechlitner was shocked by the news. Moore cautioned him not to discuss the matter with the other police officers. Of course, he knew it was a matter of time before Chilcott's suspension would be common knowledge among the Department employees.

Chapter 21

Chilcott was ordered to be at the Sheriff's Department the following morning to give a statement about the marijuana bricks found in his garage. Moore met Chilcott in the lobby at the police station and escorted him back to the main conference room. Sheriff Jackson was nervously waiting for Chilcott to arrive. Out of an abundance of caution, Jackson explained they wanted to administer a polygraph test to help determine whether Chilcott was being truthful with them. Chilcott was nervous, but reluctantly agreed. He assured Jackson and Moore that he had no reason to lie and that the test was not needed. His superiors were sympathetic, but unwilling to decline administering the test.

Several minutes later, a familiar figure appeared in the room. Chilcott recognized him as an FBI agent from the headquarters in Columbus, Ohio, who had previously conducted polygraph exams for the Department. The agent advised Chilcott that he would be placing sensors on his body to measure his autonomic arousal. Chilcott knew his heart rate, blood pressure, respiration, and skin conductivity would be measured by the device. The responses would be measured and recorded by the polygraph machine during questioning. He also knew that the FBI agent would conduct a "stimulation test", which is a demonstration of the instrument's accuracy in detecting deception.

Chilcott knew the stimulation test would be conducted first, and would become the base for evaluating when control question responses and relevant question responses would be compared. Control questions concern misdeeds that are similar to those being investigated, but refer to the subject's past and are usually broad in scope; for example, "Have you ever engaged in any criminal activity?" A person who is telling the truth is assumed to fear control questions more than relevant questions. The agent would also ask another type of question described as a relevant question. A question like, "Did you sell drugs?" would be considered a relevant question in a case like this one. Greater response to control questions signals non-deception. If no differences are found between relevant and control questions, the test result would be considered "inconclusive". The validity of polygraph tests have long been controversial and are rarely admissible in a court of law. Nevertheless, it can be used in an investigation by law enforcement officers to determine whether a suspect or witness is lying or being truthful.

Fred Jennings, the FBI agent who administered the test, started off by asking Chilcott some stimulation questions. Looking at his meter on the polygraph device he asked Chilcott, "Tell me your full name?" The indicator dial on the meter quickly spiked upward when he answered. The next question was, "Tell me your birth date?" Once again, the dial spiked upward and stopped close to where the first response had been indicated. The agent checked his notes and asked Chilcott, "What are your parents' names?" Again, the needle went upwards and landed almost in the same place as the others. The measurements were visible to Jennings on a moving graph that was displayed during the polygraph exam.

Meanwhile, Jackson and Moore watched and waited patiently for the more interesting part of the test to begin. After discovering the pot, car, and other evidence in the house, Moore had reluctantly begun to think that Chilcott was involved in the drug business with his girlfriend. The problem was he couldn't prove it. *How could an honest, hard-working policeman turn into a crook?* He'd just received two complimentary recommendations about Randy from a former neighbor and family friend, and from a county sheriff who'd known the family for years. Moore wondered if Randy's blind love for Monica had changed him from being an honest man to becoming a criminal.

The next several questions signaled an end to the stimulation questioning. Jennings marked on the graph paper where the stimulation questioning began and ended. He nodded to the Sheriff that the device seemed to be recording the responses accurately. The Sheriff nodded back signaling the agent to continue with the test. Meanwhile, Chilcott sat motionlessly in the chair and appeared to be relaxed.

Agent Jennings next question was, "Have you ever been around someone who sold drugs?" That question piqued Moore's interest as he awaited Chilcott's response.

"Yes," Chilcott said, "When I was working undercover on a multi-county drug task force." Jennings noted the response meter had a similar reading to the prior questions. From Moore's limited knowledge about polygraph exams, he understood as long as the response meter stayed within the stimulation test range the answers would be considered truthful. But if the reading on the device spiked from a response, it generally meant the person was being deceitful.

Jennings next question was, "Sergeant Chilcott, have you ever sold marijuana or any other illegal substance?"

Chilcott responded negatively, and, again, the dial stayed within the truthful range on the device.

"Sergeant Chilcott, have you ever smoked marijuana?"

Chilcott quickly responded, "Yes, while I worked undercover." The response did not vary from the other measurements.

"Were you and Monica Kerlin in business together selling marijuana?"

Chilcott's response was, "No, I was not." Once again, the dial on the device stayed within the stimulation test range, which indicated that Chilcott was still being truthful.

"Sergeant Chilcott, did you know there were blocks of unprocessed marijuana stored in your garage attic?"

"No, I did not." Once again, Jennings noted the response appeared to be truthful, according to his readings on the polygraph machine.

"Do you have any idea who put the marijuana in your garage attic?" Jennings asked.

"I have to assume my former girlfriend, Monica Kerlin, put it there," Chilcott responded.

"It's an established fact that Monica Kerlin sold drugs, is it not?"

"Yes, it is," Chilcott replied unemotionally.

"Do you know whether she sold marijuana, while using your 1983 Oldsmobile?"

"I have no such knowledge." Again, Chilcott's response registered as truthful, even though he now looked disturbed.

Jennings asked, "Did you want to add to that response, Sergeant?"

"I had no idea she was a drug dealer!" Chilcott said emphatically.

Jennings arched an eyebrow, but simply replied, "Thanks for your cooperation, Sergeant Chilcott. Before we're done here, I need to confer with Sheriff Jackson. Then, you'll be released and can go home."

Agent Jennings got up from the desk and signaled Jackson to follow him. They went out in the hall "Well Sheriff, the test indicates your sergeant is being truthful but I'm not entirely satisfied that's the case. Sergeant Chilcott could be an accomplished liar."

"Was there any indication he was lying?" Jackson asked urgently.

"As far as the test is concerned, not really," Jennings replied. "But there is something about him that makes me uncomfortable. It's mostly a gut feeling, but he was so extraordinarily calm, until the end of the examination, when he obviously wanted to convince me he did not know anything about Monica Kerlin's drug dealing. Do you really think he would know nothing about his live-in girlfriend's pot dealing, when she was even allegedly using his car to transact her business?"

Sheriff Jackson shook his head doubtfully, but didn't know what to say. There was no direct evidence linking Chilcott to Kerlin's drug dealing, and he had an impeccable record on the force.

Jennings went on, "If you want, I can continue asking more questions, but usually it only takes a few specific questions to determine if someone is lying to you. But remember Sheriff, this is not an exact science. Nevertheless, a typical polygraph exam is conclusive about 87.5% of the time, but that still leaves us with 12.5% of the results that can be wrong. A practiced liar, who has studied how to defeat the exam, may very well fool the machine." Jennings shook his head and concluded, "Sorry to leave it this way, but I'm not sure the polygraph results should be taken as definitely clearing Sergeant Chilcott of any knowledge about his girlfriend's drug dealing."

"Yes, it appears that way. But I'd hoped we'd get a more definitive idea about my officer's character after conducting the test. I've always had the highest respect for this particular officer. In fact, I even put him temporarily in charge of the Detective Bureau, for God's sake!"

"Don't be too hard on yourself, Sheriff. I've learned over the years you can never be too sure about anybody. This is a mean and deceptive society that we live in."

"Yeah, I'm ready to go back to the old days, when things weren't so complicated and people were more honest and trustworthy."

Good luck with that, thought Jennings.

Several minutes later, Jennings returned to the room and began removing the sensors from Chilcott's body. Sheriff Jackson entered the room and sternly said to Chilcott, "We're finished for now, Sergeant, but don't leave Wayne in case we need to interview you again."

After being disconnected from the polygraph device Chilcott looked at both the Sheriff and Moore, who had followed Jackson into the conference room, and said, "See, I've been telling you the truth all along. I'm disappointed you didn't believe me." Then, he abruptly walked out of the room heading for the front door of the Sheriff's Department.

Moore and Jackson looked at each other and wondered if they'd made a mistake concerning Chilcott. Regardless, they still were not finished with their investigation of Sergeant Randy Chilcott. The warrant that Jackson had received allowed them to review his bank records, savings account, CD's, checking account, and to search through his personal lock box at the Key Bank branch located in downtown Wayne. Moore had already begun preparing the necessary paperwork to make that happen.

Chilcott's automobile had already been processed in the

Sheriff's Department garage. The findings were that Monica's prints were all over the car but there were none of Chilcott's, which Moore thought was unusual. He had expected that Randy's prints would at least be found inside the vehicle. The technicians from the Ohio State Highway Patrol had examined the tires on the 1983 Oldsmobile 2-door sedan and compared the tire tread impression to the mold that had been taken at the Miller farm. To the officer's surprise, the mold was a match to Monica's left rear tire. So, with the evidence of her fingerprint at the farm the night of the murder and the tire impression indicated that Monica was there at the relevant time. Monica's status of being "a person of interest" had changed. She was now considered a bona fide suspect in the murder of the fifteen-year-old Amish girl. Moore was not totally convinced that their new found evidence necessarily meant Monica was a killer. However, Sheriff Jackson seemed more convinced that she had killed the girl.

Moore understood it was one thing to be a small-time marijuana dealer and a burglar. But it was another thing to be a killer. In his experience with the Chicago Police Department, Moore knew that it was a rare event to have a murder committed by a female. Females were normally not involved in that type of crime. Still, he remained suspicious about Chilcott and James Miller. Moore couldn't think of a viable motive or reason for Monica Kerlin to kill Rachael Miller. But he believed it was possible she had seen the girl's assailant or was aware of the person who killed her. The possible connection was the drugs. And, James had already admitted to purchasing pot from Monica Kerlin. He wondered whether there was another aspect of the investigation that he hadn't considered. *I certainly hope not,* he thought.

Chapter 22

Moore received a welcomed call from Sergeant Stanley Yoder on Thursday morning, February 2, 1989. Yoder was the officer in charge of the police garage, where Chilcott's vehicle had been towed. A routine examination of the vehicle, including lifting fingerprints from the interior and looking for drugs hidden in the vehicle, had been performed. Yoder's team also compared the mold of the tire tread returned from the FBI to the rear left wheel of Chilcott's 1983 Oldsmobile. "Surprisingly," he told Moore, "the mold and the tire tread on the Olds were a match." Yoder also informed Moore that his team made an earth-shattering discovery.

Under the driver's seat, stuck inside several seat springs, was a 25-caliber pistol with an attached sound depressor. Yoder told Moore, "The pistol was loaded and was recently fired." It was discovered when a tall officer tried to adjust the seat backwards when moving the vehicle out of the police garage. The seat was sticking, so he looked under the seat to see what the problem was and noticed the weapon. The officer used rubber gloves to remove the weapon out from under the seat.

"Holy shit! I'll be right there," Moore said as he got up and hurriedly walked to the garage.

When Detective Moore arrived in the garage, Yoder was there waiting for him. "The weapon is on the work bench over there," he said pointing at the bench. Moore put on his rubber gloves and carefully inspected the weapon. He'd seen this type of handgun when he was on the force in Chicago. It was a cheaply manufactured 25-caliber weapon. Raven Arms manufactured the MP-25. Moore noted that the serial number was unreadable. *Probably scratched off with a grinder,* he thought. An obviously hand-made silencer was attached to the gun's barrel. He noted the weapon was loaded with three 25 ACP rounds. Moore knew the gun's magazine held six. He wondered, *So, what happened to the other three?* Moore examined the MP-25 for fingerprints, but the gun appeared clean. He assumed the gun was wiped clean by whoever used it last. *Was that Monica or Chilcott?*

Moore recollected that he had only noticed 22 rounds fired into Chilcott's basement firing range. He hoped that fact indicated the MP-25 was Monica's and not Randy's. But, after finding the weapon hidden under Chilcott's car seat, Randy had to be brought back for another interview.

According to the gun registration information received from the Ohio State Highway Patrol, Chilcott was the owner of just one handgun. It was the 22-caliber Smith and Wesson that was stored in his basement and locked away in the cabinet. Maybe the 25-caliber weapon had been fired at the target range as well. *Should he ask Chilcott to allow him access to the basement again, without a search*

warrant? If Chilcott refused, that might indicate something important was overlooked during the previous search, and maybe, Chilcott was aware of it.

At 10:00 a.m., Moore called Chilcott at home. The phone rang several times before Chilcott answered sounding as if he'd been asleep. "Hello," he said dully.

"Did I wake you up, Randy?" Moore asked.

"Not really, I've just been watching a boring television show. What can I do for you?" Chilcott replied coolly.

"I'm just calling to tell you we're done examining your car. I could bring it back to you this afternoon. If I did, would you be able to take me back to the Sheriff's department or should I have a deputy follow me to your home?" Moore asked politely.

"Did you find out anything about the tire tread? Did it match with the mold that we made at the farm?" Chilcott asked curiously.

"You know I can't talk about an ongoing investigation."

"Of course; sorry, I forgot," Chilcott said sounding annoyed.

"Look, Randy, I don't make the rules. I just try to follow them."

"I know," Chilcott replied. And trying to sound more amicable, said, "Yeah, if you can bring the car back after 3:00 p.m., that would work for me."

"Can you drive me back to the station?"

"Sure, I'll be glad to do it. No need to tie up another officer."

"Great, see you at 3:00 p.m. And thanks, Randy," Moore said courteously.

Following his conversation with Chilcott, Moore contacted Sheriff Jackson and apprised him of the new development in the case. After bagging the handgun and marking it as evidence, Moore returned to his office and locked the handgun away in his filing cabinet. Then, he went to Jackson's office and shared his next move with his boss. Moore said that he planned to return the car to Chilcott that afternoon. And, when he arrived at Chilcott's residence, he'd ask him if it would be alright to go down to the basement. Assuming Chilcott approved, he planned to tell him he needed to take several more photographs of the area. But instead of taking pictures, he told Jackson, he planned to reexamine the target area more carefully and look for any sign of a 25-caliber hole in the 4x4 target board.

Moore explained that, at the time of the search, he thought the holes in the target were made by 22-caliber projectiles. But, he admitted to Jackson, that he could have been mistaken. Another inspection should reveal whether there were also 25-caliber holes as well. Moore also told Jackson that when Chilcott drove him back to the Sheriff's Department, he was planning to tell Randy that they needed to ask him several more questions. Jackson agreed it was a good plan and he could hardly wait to hear Chilcott's response when questioned about the 25-caliber handgun found in his car.

Following his conversation with Sheriff Jackson, Moore returned to his office and resumed the search to locate the Kerlin women. Most people can be found by referring to telephone books, voter registration information with the County Clerk, property tax records, IRS or state department of revenue records, parole records, or vehicle registration information. Moore noted that Chilcott previously indicated he tried all those sources to locate Monica and her mother, Dorothy Kerlin. Supposedly, they were residing in the Charleston, West Virginia, area. Unfortunately, his search was not successful.

Moore knew there were other ways to find people, such as, talking to their relatives, friends, past neighbors, or employers. He was aware that Monica had few friends or neighbors to contact and that she was not employed. Moore also was aware that she had a former spouse. His name was Billy Slidell and an ex-con from Wheeling, West Virginia. Moore tried to find Slidell's telephone number, but was unsuccessful.

He called the parole office in Ohio County, West Virginia and was referred to Lloyd Hurtt, Slidell's parole officer. Hurtt told Moore that Slidell had missed the last several appointments and there was a warrant out for his arrest. Candidly, Hurtt admitted it was hard to find his type, if Slidell didn't want to be found. Moore thanked him and hung up the phone. He couldn't believe his bad luck, but vowed to keep searching for the Kerlins.

In the meantime, Moore was swamped with a larger caseload due to Chilcott's absence. Deputy Sheriff Howard Lechlitner's status was changed from temporary to a full-

time basis to help with some of those investigations. But then, Moore had to spend time bringing Lechlitner up to speed on what he needed to do on the cases assigned to him. Fortunately, in January 1989 the incidence of criminal activity in upper northwestern Ohio decreased by 5% over the same time period in 1988. The decrease lessened the burden on Moore of trying to solve crimes in Grant County. *I hope I can bring this Miller investigation to a successful completion,* he thought. He knew there were other cases waiting that needed his attention.

Around 2:40 p.m. Moore got into Chilcott's 1983 Oldsmobile Cutlass, started the engine, and drove to Chilcott's home. Moore noted that the Olds was pretty sound and drove well. He pulled into the driveway as the two-car garage door opened. Obviously, Chilcott was waiting for him in the garage. Moore drove the vehicle into the garage and parked in an empty space. He turned off the motor and stepped out of the car. Chilcott was standing off to the side by the door into the house.

Chilcott noticed with surprise that Moore had a 35 mm Nikon camera swung over his shoulder. "What's the camera for?" Chilcott asked curiously.

"Well, I hoped you'd allow me to go down to the basement again and take a few more pictures. I forgot to do it when we searched your house."

"I guess that's alright," Chilcott said unenthusiastically. "Go ahead, you know where to go."

"Thanks, Randy. It will only take me a few minutes and I'll be done."

Chilcott didn't respond, so Moore went inside and then down the stairs to the basement shooting range. He looked over the hanging target once again and didn't see any difference in the size of the holes in the wooden target. But just as he started to head back up the stairs, he looked up and saw a slug sticking out through one of the floor joists. He quickly removed it with his pocket knife and placed the slug inside his shirt pocket. Moore didn't think it was a 22-caliber slug. He quickly flashed a couple pictures and then returned to the living room, where Chilcott was sitting in front of the television set.

Chilcott turned off the television set and led Moore back into the garage. They seated themselves in the Olds with Chilcott behind the wheel.

On the way to the Sheriff's Department, while they were engaged in casual conversation, Moore asked in an innocent tone of voice, "Hey, I forgot to ask you, Randy, what did you do during the New Year's Holiday weekend?

Chilcott's hands tightened on the wheel. He sensed a menacing motive behind Moore's nonchalant tone. *Maybe he's trying to determine if I had something to do with Monica's disappearance.* But trying to maintain a normal tone in his own voice, Chilcott responded, "Well, let's see; uh, you know Clarence, we went out to dinner on New Year's Eve, had a few drinks, and returned home. The rest of the weekend, I watched football, ate, drank, and got ready to go back to work."

Moore nodded, but didn't reply.

When they arrived at the Sheriff's Department, Moore

asked Chilcott to come inside. He explained that there were a few more questions they wanted to ask him and that it wouldn't take very long. Chilcott agreed, but was then surprised and a little alarmed when Moore gave him another Miranda warning.

Moore said gruffly, "Our questioning won't take long and you know the procedure."

"Yes, of course I do, Captain, Sir," Chilcott said irritably.

The questioning began with Moore stating, "Randy, you'll never believe what we found in your vehicle under the front seat." Chilcott didn't respond at first and immediately began to look nervous. Moore sensed that Chilcott knew where this was leading.

But after a few seconds, Chilcott regained his composure and asked in a casual tone, "What did you find, Captain?"

"We found a 25-caliber handgun, loaded, with a sound depressor attached to the barrel of the gun. And, there were only three bullets left in the magazine. Does the gun belong to you?" Moore asked sternly.

"I have no idea what you're talking about Captain," Chilcott said with a look of honest concern on his face. "I don't know how it got there. Maybe it belonged to Monica. Maybe it was there when I purchased the vehicle. Up until now, I didn't even know it existed. Maybe you ought to ask Monica if you want to know about the gun." Chilcott met Moore's gaze squarely. He sounded surprised and annoyed.

"Yes, we will be sure to ask her, once we've located her," Moore said. "So, if I'm to understand you correctly, you're saying the 25-caliber gun was never in your home and was never fired in your basement. Is that correct?"

"Well, to the best of my knowledge, no, it was never in my home."

"Thanks for your cooperation, Randy. For the moment, you're free to go," Moore replied calmly. He watched as Chilcott quickly rose from the chair and strolled out of the room.

As usual, Sheriff Jackson had listened in the observation room to the brief examination of Chilcott. As soon as Chilcott left, Jackson entered the small interrogation room and asked Moore whether he believed Chilcott's story. Moore scratched his head and then responded slowly, "I'm not sure. It could be a gun he found during a prior investigation, but failed to turn in. However, it could be his former girlfriend's gun. I guess we'll see. I'm very hopeful we'll get another clue and be able to find Monica and put her behind bars on the marijuana charges. Then we can question her about the handgun found under the front seat. Once that information is obtained, I can proceed with the homicide investigation of the Amish girl."

The course of this investigation is certainly taking puzzling turns, Moore thought. *What's the connection between the weapon, Monica, and the Amish girl? Is Chilcott involved? How does the weed fit in with the murder? This is certainly one of the strangest cases I've ever been involved with.*

Chapter 23

The Tennessee Highway Patrol received a frantic call from a hiker in the late afternoon of Friday, February 17, 1989. The distraught man claimed to have found the remains of a human being buried in a wooded area. The body was wrapped in a black plastic tarp and covered by a mixture of dirt and small rocks just off I-75. The man's hiking companion and pet, "Sam", a three-year-old German shepherd, was following him on a mountainous trail through a dense forest area. Sam stopped to smell something interesting buried in the floor of the woods. The hiker, Don Abernathy, called for the dog to come, but his command was ignored. When Abernathy approached the site, he smelled a terrible noxious odor the closer he got to Sam. He discovered that Sam had found a body partially buried in the ground.

The Tennessee Highway Patrol in Knoxville and the Campbell County Sheriff's Department in Caryville, Tennessee were called to the burial site. A Campbell County Sheriff's deputy arrived in less than twenty minutes and began to process the crime scene. Twenty minutes later the Tennessee Highway Patrol arrived at the remote site to assist the Sheriff's deputy. They found a body wrapped in black plastic buried in a dense woods which was part of the Cumberland Trail State Park.

Cumberland Trail serves as a natural preserve, filled with dense forests, mountain peaks, scenic views, fields, and multiple hiking trails. The Park is open year-round and receives many visitors who enjoy the overlooks, hiking trails, mountain bike paths, and a vast landscape of lakes and streams to the south. Part of the Cumberland Trail State Park is located about 12 miles south from the Kentucky/Tennessee border. Conceived as a long-distance hiking trail, the 300-mile Cumberland Trail is the only linear park in Tennessee. The trail serves as a resource for many types of recreational activities, including hiking, backpacking, exploring, rock climbing, trail running, bird watching, water sports, and fishing.

The investigators believed from the look of the burial site and the condition of the body that the corpse had been there over a month. Winter had come early to the Appalachian Mountain range and the ground froze unseasonably early. Caryville and the Cumberland Trail State Park were within the East Tennessee Mountains near the base of the Appalachian range. Due to the hardness of the ground the police officers assumed the assailant(s) were barely able to dig an adequate hole for the remains. The investigators theorized that the killer(s) had to use a pick to break up the mixture of rock and dirt before using a shovel to finish digging the shallow hole. The grave was covered with dirt, small rocks, fallen tree limbs, and leaves.

Caryville is known for its rolling hills, beautiful mountains, streams, and lakes. It's a good location to catch an abundant number of fish. Wild game were plentiful in the mountains and in the dense woods north of Caryville. The town of Caryville is situated in a valley between the Cross Mountain to the west and a series of rugged hills to the east. Cove Lake State Park is immediately north of the town. The town was founded in the mid 1880's and named after a prominent local landowner. Its population is around 2,000. The town boomed quickly as a construction camp for the railroad back in the day.

Shortly after the local police officers arrived and began working the case the special forensics investigators from the Tennessee Highway Patrol office in Knoxville were called in take over the investigation. The body was taken to the Knoxville, Tennessee morgue located in the basement of the University of Tennessee Medical Center. The Knoxville coroner performed a complete forensics autopsy. DNA and fingerprint samples were sent to the FBI for identification. The autopsy revealed the young woman, believed to be in her mid to late twenties, was shot twice in the head execution style. She'd also been shot once directly in the heart. She died from the shot to the heart. The pathologist claimed she had bled out quickly. The body was wrapped in a 6 by 8-foot plastic tarp, which is available for purchase in any hardware store. Heavy-duty grey duct tape was used to secure the corpse inside the tarp. The assailant(s) wrapped the tarp and sealed it with three sections of tape around the corpse's head, waist, and leg area.

* * *

The body was identified by investigators from the FBI in Quantico, Virginia on March 8, 1989. The remains were identified as Monica Kerlin, whose last known address was in Wayne, Ohio. Immediately, the FBI notified the Grant County Sheriff's Department in Ohio and that's how Captain Moore was made aware of her death.

Moore conferred with Sheriff Roger Jackson and Prosecutor Samuel Murphy, and the decision was made to apprehend Randy Chilcott and arrest him for the aggravated murder (1st degree murder) of Monica Kerlin and for drug related charges on account of the marijuana found on his premises. An hour later, Chilcott was in the interrogation room at the Sheriff's Department being questioned. The arresting officers indicated to Moore that Chilcott had been Mirandized.

When Moore opened the door to the interrogation room, he saw Chilcott slumped over on the edge of the hard-wood chair. His handcuffs had been removed and there was a small plastic water bottle on the desk in front of him. The bottle appeared to be unopened. Moore said, "Hello Sergeant," his tone was tinged with disbelief, bitterness, and regret.

Chilcott looked up and noticed Moore in the room, but he made no response.

Moore began his questioning by saying, "I suppose, you realize you've been accused of committing a capital offense. First-degree aggravated murder is a very serious charge. You're also being charged with possession and intent to distribute over four pounds of an illicit drug. Those are felony charges on top of the murder charge you face. If you tell me everything that happened, the Prosecutor told me he would be open to making a deal." Moore studied Chilcott, who appeared to be unaffected by his comments.

Chilcott continued to gaze down at the floor and remain silent.

Moore pressed on with his questions. "I know you're probably aware of the differences between the two murder charges, Randy, but let me refresh your memory. Aggravated murder gets you either life imprisonment or a lethal injection, whereas murder allows for parole and a variety of sentences. You might only serve ten to twenty years and you'd be a free man. If you tell me the truth about what really happened and give me a signed statement, I'll use every bit of influence I have to see that the aggravated murder charge is dropped."

Chilcott remained silent, while Moore awaited his response. After a minute or so, Chilcott raised his head, looked into Moore's eyes, and said, "I'd like to see an attorney."

Moore closed his file folder, got up from his wooden chair, and said, "If you change your mind, Randy, let me know." He left the room. Two Grant County Deputy sheriffs entered the room, handcuffed Chilcott, and escorted him out of the room. Moore knew that he'd be incarcerated in the newly renovated Grant County Jail on the opposite side of the building.

Several hours later, Moore visited Chilcott in his cell. He told him that a judge had agreed to temporarily assign a lawyer from the public defender's office to represent him. The lawyer's name was, Willard Berry, a well-known local attorney. He also told Chilcott to expect to meet Berry the following morning at his pre-trial hearing.

Chilcott thanked Moore and then lay back on top of his uncomfortable jailhouse mattress and tried to fall asleep.

Chapter 24

Breakfast was doled out to Chilcott and the other prisoners in the Grant County Jail every day at 5:30 a.m. Henry Jefferson, a black inmate trustee, brought three unsavory meals a day for the inmates to eat. Prior to his arrival at each cell in the jail, the inmates knew he was approaching by the sound of his cart's squeaky wheels. For his protection Chilcott was separated from the general population, because he was a former police officer. So, he had a jail cell all to himself.

Just before 8:00 a.m., two Sheriff's deputies appeared at Chilcott's cell, unlocked the cell door, and entered the cell. They handcuffed Chilcott's wrists and ankles and led him to a police transport vehicle. The police van was to deliver him and several other inmates to the Grant County Courthouse for their pre-trial hearings. The reality of being charged with a felony was beginning to sink in to Randy Chilcott. He felt nervous, vulnerable, and fearful.

When the van arrived at the side entrance to the courthouse, the officers unlocked and opened the door, and then led Chilcott and the other detainees to the courtroom on the second floor. However, Chilcott was escorted into a small room adjacent to the courtroom. He was instructed to take a seat while they waited for Willard Berry, Chilcott's assigned attorney, to show up. Upon the attorney's arrival, the officers left the room.

Willard Berry worked with the public defender's office for many years. He was a capable attorney, when he wasn't drinking too much. His drinking problem resulted in a temporary license suspension. But, after a year of therapy, Berry was able to resume practicing law. He had always preferred representing and defending the poor and down-trodden members of society. So, he applied for and received a position with the Grant County Public Defender's Office.

If given a choice, Willard Berry would not have selected Randy Chilcott as a client. Berry was short, overweight, with graying blond hair. He was born and raised in southern Mississippi and had come to Wayne to care for Mary Berry, his unmarried, older sister. Berry had a noticeable southern accent.

When the attorney entered the counsel room, where his client was waiting, he was carrying a briefcase and a cup of coffee. When the middle-aged attorney opened his briefcase, Chilcott could see there were several file folders inside. Berry greeted Chilcott without emotion and removed a file folder from inside his briefcase. He placed the folder on the table and sat across from Chilcott. Berry opened the file folder, which contained all the documents and information he had received pertaining to Chilcott's criminal case. After studying the contents of the file folder for a few minutes, Berry turned his attention to Chilcott and said, "I'm Willard Berry. Judge Lawrence Wilson, who is the presiding judge on your case, assigned me to represent you at your arraignment this morning. If you are unable to retain a private attorney and the Court determines that you qualify for representation by the Public Defender's Office for your case, then I'll be your lawyer. However, if you are able to retain private counsel, and do so, then I will withdraw as your attorney. Do you understand what my role will be for you at this preliminary hearing?"

"Uh, yes, I guess so," Chilcott replied.

"Now, it is possible, given what I've seen in the file, especially given your status as a deputy sheriff and a clean record, that you will be offered a plea bargain by the prosecuting attorney. If that occurs before you retain private counsel, then-"

"I can't afford one," Chilcott said disconsolately, interrupting Berry.

"Well, that's a decision for the judge, but let's proceed with dealing with what we need to accomplish this morning. Can you tell me whether you have an alibi for the crimes you've been charged with?"

"Mr. Berry, I'm not guilty," Chilcott responded without delay.

"Well then, this hearing should go pretty easily. You'll tell the judge you're pleading not guilty and that you want a jury trial. He'll accept your plea and set a trial date about six months from now. He probably won't grant you bail, because of the murder charge, but do you want me to ask for it anyway?" Berry inquired.

"Yes, please ask about bail. If the judge grants it, I'll be surprised. But it would be nice to know how much money I'd have to come up with. I'm sure I couldn't come up with enough money to pay a bail bondsman to gain my release. Still, it would be nice to know what it would take."

"Alright, I'll give it a try. As a first offender and a former law enforcement officer, the judge might grant bail. We'll never know unless we ask."

"Yeah, but he probably won't grant any bail request. He'd probably prefer to throw the book at me, because I'm a cop," Chilcott said sadly.

"Yes, he might," Berry replied and eyed his client cautiously. "So, uh, we have about fifteen more minutes to wait before your hearing begins. Do you need anything? Are your jailers keeping you segregated from the rest of the prisoners?"

"No, I don't need anything. And, yes, I am segregated from the rest of the prisoners," Chilcott answered.

"Good," Berry said.

Ten minutes later, the two deputies came back into the room, checked Chilcott's hands and ankle cuffs, and announced, "It's time for your hearing, please come with us." The officers led Chilcott into the courtroom and placed him near the back corner of the room. "Keep your mouth shut until the judge calls your name," one of the officers said. Chilcott did as he was told.

Judge Wilson sat on an elevated platform in a high-backed, black cloth-appointed chair behind the bench, which was a long, dark wood desk with a gavel in the middle and a brass model of a scale of justice at one end and pile of case files on the other end. Situated ten feet away from the judge's bench were two rectangular tables with six feet separating the tables. Behind each of the tables and facing toward the bench were two swivel chairs. After waiting five minutes, Chilcott heard his name called and was escorted to the front of the room and told to take his place beside Attorney Berry, who was standing behind the right chair at the table on the left side of the courtroom. Chilcott stood behind the other chair to the left of his attorney. The prosecuting attorney sat at the other table with a paralegal assistant at his side. Circuit Court Judge Wilson peered over his spectacles at Berry and Chilcott. Then he looked down at the materials in the case file bearing the title, State of Ohio v. Randall T. Chilcott.

Judge Wilson then looked sternly at Chilcott and said, "In reviewing your financial history and lack of assets, Mr. Chilcott, I've determined that you cannot afford to hire an attorney yourself. You are no longer employed, you have no assets or property of significant value, and you have no current income. Therefore, I'm instructing the public defender's office to assign you an attorney. I see Mr. Berry at your side and that he has filed his appearance to represent you at this arraignment hearing. So, unless the Public Defender's Office has reason to assign another lawyer to your case, I'll assume Mr. Berry will serve as your legal counsel at this hearing and going forward. Is that acceptable to you, Mr. Chilcott?"

"Yes, thank you, Your Honor," Chilcott responded.

Judge Wilson nodded at Willard Berry and intoned, "You may be seated." Chilcott quickly sat down beside his defense attorney. Judge Wilson handed the file over to the bailiff, who was standing off to the side of the bench. The bailiff announced in a loud voice the defendant's name and case number, and ordered Chilcott to stand for the formal reading of the charges against him. The bailiff handed the file back to Judge Wilson, who read through the charges, informed the defendant of the minimum and maximum sentence for each of the charged offenses, and droned through a list of the defendant's rights, including the right to counsel, to a speedy trial, a jury of his peers, to confront his accusers, etc. Finally, Judge Wilson asked Chilcott, "How do you plead to the charges of aggravated murder, possession of an illicit drug, and intent to distribute, guilty or not-guilty?"

Chilcott immediately said, "Not guilty, Your Honor."

"Alright, Mr. Chilcott," Judge Wilson replied. "Do you want a jury trial or not?"

"I'd like a jury trial, Your Honor."

Wilson checked his trial book and said, "The earliest trial date that I can give you is the day after Labor Day on Tuesday, September 5, 1989. Will that work for your schedule, Mr. Berry?"

Berry quickly looked at his pocket calendar, and then replied, "Yes, Judge, it will."

"Fine, the trial is set for 8:00 a.m., September 5, 1989."

Judge Wilson picked up his gavel, but before he could wield it, Berry spoke up, "Your Honor, the issue of bail –

my client requests that a reasonable bail be granted considering he's a first-time offender."

Without hesitation, Judge Wilson responded, "Request denied. Mr. Chilcott, you will be remanded to the Grant County Jail until you're either convicted of the charges against you or your acquitted. This hearing is concluded," Judge Wilson said as he pounded his gavel on the bench ending the proceedings.

Berry looked over at Chilcott and said, "I'll be reviewing the evidence the police have produced on your case. Once I have a good grasp of the evidence against you, I'll visit you again at the jail to discuss plans for your defense. Does that sound alright to you?"

"Yes, but if you have any questions, Mr. Berry, please let me know."

"I will, Randy." Berry patted his client on the shoulder, pursed his lips, and nodded.

Detective Moore was in the courtroom sitting behind the prosecuting attorney's table throughout the hearing. Afterwards, he stood at the prosecutor's table and commented to Prosecutor Murphy, "I'm expecting to uncover more evidence prior to the trial. Hopefully, we can wrap this case up in short order and send a bad cop to jail."

"Well, so far we have compiled a lot of circumstantial evidence. From my experience as a prosecuting attorney, it is harder to get a conviction without an eye witness to the crime or having a signed confession from the defendant. As you know, we have neither. Unfortunately, I may end up having to make a deal with Randy Chilcott, even though I don't want to. But we'll see how the case develops as we work through the formal discovery phase. There are a few witness statements I want to tie down more tightly through depositions."

"I'll do my best to find more concrete evidence for you to use," Moore replied. "I'm going back to work. I need to study Kerlin's autopsy report. Maybe there's something there that I can glean from the report to help bolster our case against Chilcott."

"Good luck, Detective," Murphy replied as he turned back to the counsel table and picked up his next case file.

"Thank you," Moore uttered distractedly as he watched the police officers escort Chilcott out of the courtroom. *Randy, I know you're guilty of murder. And hopefully, I'll be able to help prove it,* Moore thought.

* * *

Moore arrived at his office early Friday morning, March 10, 1989, to try to resolve some of the less important cases he was responsible for. He'd felt the pressure of dealing with mounting criminal cases ever since Chilcott was suspended and then charged. Moore was working on the Rachael Miller case, the Monica Kerlin case, and four other cases involving less serious crimes. His replacement for Chilcott, Deputy Sheriff Howard Lechlitner, was finally getting up to speed. Thankfully, Lechlitner was taking up some of the slack in Chilcott's absence. That allowed Moore to concentrate most of his time on the two more serious investigations.

Sitting at his desk, Moore thought about the evidence that he'd compiled against Chilcott. He'd found a spent 25-caliber slug in the floor joist just above the target in Chilcott's basement shooting range. That slug matched one of the two 25-caliber slugs found in Monica Kerlin's head during the autopsy. There was the 25-caliber handgun found under the seat in Randy Chilcott's 1983 Oldsmobile Cutlass that proved to be the murder weapon. However, there was no 25-caliber weapon registered to Randy Chilcott. Assuming Chilcott did kill Monica Kerlin, Moore was finding it hard to come up with a motive. There were several possible motives in the case, he thought. *Perhaps it had something to do with the marijuana business. Maybe there was a disagreement over how to split the profit from the sales.*

Chilcott had told Moore that on January 24, 1989 he had taken Monica Kerlin to the bus stop in Wayne. But that would have been a month after Christmas, which was when her supposed bus trip to Charleston, West Virginia had taken place. Chilcott claimed his relationship with Monica Kerlin was faltering and that she'd decided to temporarily stay with her mother in West Virginia. But on February 17, 1989, a hiker found Monica Kerlin's body in a shallow grave near Caryville, Tennessee, which is a distance of over 350 miles away from Charleston, West Virginia. Moore wondered whether Chilcott had killed Monica Kerlin in Wayne, Ohio or elsewhere and buried her body sometime between December 30, 1988 and January 1, 1989 near Caryville, Tennessee.

Moore calculated the approximate mileage from Wayne, Ohio to Caryville, Tennessee and determined it was roughly 480 miles. Chilcott's 1983 Oldsmobile Cutlass Supreme engine was a V-6. He calculated that at a normal driving speed of 60 MPH and with an 18-gallon gas tank, Chilcott would have had to fill up the gas tank prior to leaving on the trip from Wayne, Ohio. And, he would have needed to refill the tank twice before returning to Wayne from Tennessee. Since Chilcott was a big NASCAR enthusiast, he assumed Chilcott would prefer Sunoco gas. Sunoco was the gasoline of choice for NASCAR fans.

Moore obtained the gasoline sales records from the local Sunoco station in Wayne and discovered that Chilcott filled up his tank around 8:30 a.m. on January 1, 1989. He filled up again in the late afternoon of January 2, 1989. Chilcott had never mentioned he was taking a vacation over the holiday weekend. So, why would he need to fill his tank twice in two days? Besides, he claimed to have been home on New Year's Day.

On a hunch, Moore asked for the assistance of the Ohio State Highway Patrol to check for video surveillance tape recordings from any Sunoco Service Station in the Cincinnati area directly off of I-75. The distance between Wayne and Cincinnati was approximately 250 miles. The drive time would be a little over 4 hours. Moore figured most people would stop every 4 hours for gasoline, to use the toilet, get some food or drink to snack on, and to stretch. He was hoping for a miracle, because the circumstantial evidence might not be enough to get Chilcott convicted by a jury. Without a confession or an

eye witness to murder, things could be difficult. *If I can find a video of Chilcott and Kerlin together in the Oldsmobile at a service station away from Wayne during the relevant time period, that could be huge!* The forensic team was unable to locate a tire print near the burial site just across the Tennessee/Kentucky border in rural Tennessee. So, that path seemed to be closed for the moment.

* * *

A few weeks after seeking assistance from the Ohio State Highway Patrol, Moore got a call from an officer. The officer had found a video-tape recording made during the New Year's holiday weekend. A Sunoco service station owner just north of the Kentucky line stored his recorded video tapes for three months before reusing them. After three months, he'd collect them and reuse them again in the recording devices maintained in various spots that monitored the service station on a 24/7 basis. After looking at many video tapes, an Ohio State patrolman discovered Chilcott's vehicle being filled up with gasoline around 1:00 p.m. on January 1, 1989 at a Sunoco station right off of I-75 south of downtown Cincinnati.

The license plate on the 1983 Olds was clearly visible and matched Chilcott's plate. The vehicle in the video tape was Chilcott's 83 Oldsmobile. The driver of the vehicle was a man. There was no one riding in the passenger seat. Moore requested a copy of the tape recording and was able to identify the driver as Randy Chilcott. Detective Moore thought it was interesting that Chilcott claimed he was in Wayne the entire New Year's weekend. Moore figured New Year's Day was the only time available for Chilcott to have gone to Tennessee, bury Monica's body, and return home the same day. Moore had an eye witness report that Chilcott and Kerlin were seen eating and drinking in Wayne on New Year's Eve between the hours of 7:00 p.m. and 11:30 p.m. That was the last time they were seen together.

I've finally found several more pieces of evidence for the prosecutor to use, Moore thought. With the tape recording, gas purchase tickets, 25-caliber weapon, and the 25-caliber slug found in Chilcott's basement matching the 25-caliber slug removed from Kerlin's head, well, Moore hoped that would be enough to obtain a conviction.

Moore excitedly informed Prosecutor Murphy of the video-tape evidence he'd obtained. Murphy also got excited as he listened to Captain Moore describe the New Year's Day video tape. But he cautioned Moore that the evidence he had obtained still might not be enough to ensure a conviction. Murphy said, "An attorney worth his salt could dispute most of the evidence compiled thus far." Chilcott could be in trouble for lying to the police, but that was not a capital offense. But an eye witness report of Chilcott killing Monica Kerlin or a confession to the crime would be preferred to ensure Chilcott got life imprisonment or a lethal injection as punishment for committing the crime of murder.

Chapter 25

Two weeks had passed since Chilcott's court hearing had taken place. His attorney, Willard Berry, visited him once since the hearing and asked him several questions and quickly left. Being incarcerated wouldn't have been too bad, but the isolation was killing Chilcott. There were no people to talk to other than the guards.

Chilcott looked around the small jail cell. It was barely big enough for two inmates. Inside the cell there was a small window, a sink, a toilet, and one set of bunk beds. He slept on the lower bunk. The jail stunk of human filth, where more than two dozen persons were locked up. Ward 'A' contained most of the harden criminals waiting for trial. Ward 'B' was for dunks and those who committed less serious crimes. But ward "B" was where Chilcott was housed. Chilcott wondered, how long would it take to make him totally stir-crazy existing under these conditions.

His mornings consisted of getting up, relieving himself, washing his face, and brushing his teeth. Prisoners were allowed to shower twice a week. Chilcott thought that the Grant County Jail served the most disgusting and tasteless food available. The food was pretty much the same for lunch and dinner. The only dish he anticipated with any enthusiasm was the occasional serving of roast beef. For some reason the roast beef didn't taste nearly as rancid as some of the other dinner choices served at 5:00 p.m. For entertainment Chilcott could read a book, work a puzzle, or write a letter. Chilcott chose to sleep most of the time between meals. The days seemed to pass ever so slowly.

Chilcott couldn't sleep soundly at night. Early one morning he heard the sounds of a scuffle approaching his cell and a man was yelling obscenities. Chilcott assumed the yelling was directed at the guards. The noise continued until he heard a cell door open and heard the noise of a man being thrown into the cell next to his. Then, he heard one of the guards say, "Welcome back to the Grant County Jail, asshole," as the cell door slammed shut. The prisoner yelled back another obscenity as the guards walked away chuckling. Chilcott thought it was close to 4:30 a.m., but he didn't know for sure. His wrist watch was confiscated when he was processed into the jail. He tried to go back to sleep, but he was wide awake.

An hour later, he heard a voice penetrate the cement wall that separated the cells. "Anybody next door?" the cantankerous voice asked.

Chilcott quickly responded, "I'm Randy. Do you have a name?"

"I'm Carlisle, but my friends call me Red Bone. What you in for Randy?"

"A couple of charges," Chilcott replied.

"Are you a bad ass?"

"Not really."

"If you're not a bad ass, are you one of the fellows," the voice asked chuckling.

"I'm neither. Besides, I'm innocent of the charges!" Chilcott blurted out passionately.

"Sure, you are, Randy," Carlisle replied. "Don't tell those pricks otherwise and stick to your story."

"I will. So, why are you in here?" Chilcott asked.

"They say I was drunk and knocked out some guy's front teeth in a bar fight last night. I tried to explain, but that didn't work out. Yeah, they never believe me," Carlisle said with a cynical laugh. "The prick filed a complaint against me and I've been charged with assault, disorderly conduct, public intoxication, and resisting arrest."

"That's understandable, you were drunk."

"Well, maybe. Say, did you hear about the cop they arrested for murdering his girlfriend and dumping her body in Tennessee?"

"Uh, yeah, I'm that guy," Chilcott replied reluctantly. "I suppose the story is all over the news."

"Yup. Between the television broadcasts, newspaper articles, and talk on the street, you're kinda infamous." Carlisle paused, then asked, "Did the bitch cheat on you? Is that why you killed her?"

"I told you before, I didn't do it." Chilcott ground his teeth in angry frustration.

"Okay, sure, I believe you, if that's gonna be your

story," Carlisle said, all the while thinking to himself, *Sure, you're as innocent as Jeffrey Dahmer was, but the difference is you're not a serial killer. And, you don't eat your victims.*

Quickly changing the subject, Chilcott asked, "Why do your friends call you Red Bone?"

"Because I'm an American Indian. Hell, my brother's an Indian chief, but I'm just a brave. I've only got one feather in my war bonnet," he admitted with a laugh.

"You're shitting me, aren't you?"

"No, it's true! The cops think I'm crazy, but I'm really not. I just like messing with people. You know, I went to the college of hard knocks and I got me a degree in harassment and BS. And I'm damn proud of it."

"Really!" For the first time since his incarceration, Chilcott felt a moment of pleasure. His new jailhouse buddy, the strange character, who called himself Red Bone, entertained him.

"I told you that I wasn't crazy, but I have papers to prove otherwise. A few years ago, I was incarcerated in a nut house for several months."

"How did that work out for you?"

"Well, better than I expected. If you want good drugs, that's where you go to get them. I can attest to that," Red Bone said smiling to himself with satisfaction.

A minute later, breakfast arrived. Chilcott called out to Carlisle, "Hope you enjoy your breakfast. Looks like we're having a deluxe meal this morning," Chilcott said looking with distaste at the oat meal and eggs on the plate the trustee had passed to him.

“Looks like what they feed the hogs! I’m not very hungry,” Carlisle replied.

“Suit yourself, but I’m going to eat and then take a short nap. I’ll talk to you later,” Chilcott said.

“No problem, Randy. I’ll talk to you later.”

An hour had passed when Chilcott heard, “Are you awake yet?”

Chilcott responded, “I am now.” He wondered whether his buddy next door was going to turn out to be more of an annoyance than a jailhouse friend.

“Hey, I’ve been thinking about your situation. You know you’re going to die by lethal injection, if you’re convicted of aggravated murder. Probably lucky though, they say it’s more humane.”

That thoroughly annoyed Chilcott, so he answered angrily, “Carlisle, would you please shut the hell up and let me rest.”

“Hey Randy, don’t get so upset. It’s not good for you. Did you forget to take your medicine this morning?”

“Carlisle, just leave me the hell alone. I’m not in the mood for your crap!”

“Yeah, go ahead. I was just trying to make conversation. Did you know that prior to lethal injection they used the electric chair. I heard a fellow named Thomas Edison invented the contraption, but I’m not sure.

I think he had a laboratory somewhere in New Jersey."

"Thanks for the history lesson, but I'm going back to sleep."

"Yeah, no problem."

Later that day, but before supper was served, Carlisle called out, "Randy are you awake?"

"What do you want now?" Chilcott answered crossly.

"Did you know executions are carried out in Lucasville, Ohio, at the Southern Ohio Correctional Facility? But don't worry, as long as you file an appeal, you'll probably serve about 15 years before you're executed. If you don't file an appeal, you could be dead in six months from the end of your trial."

That sent a chill down Randy's spine, but he forced himself to respond with a controlled voice. "How do you know about all this stuff?"

"I watch a lot of crime shows on television."

After listening to Carlisle for less than a day, Chilcott was wondering if he should complain to the guards about being harassed. *Probably wouldn't do me any good,* he thought.

But before the guards turned the lights out for the evening, Carlisle was at it again. "Hey Randy!"

"Yeah, what do you want now?" Chilcott replied irritably. *Here we go again,* he thought.

"Don't be upset with me. I'm just trying to help you."

"What is it then?"

"I've been thinking."

My God, that could be dangerous, thought Chilcott. "What now? Are you going to ask me about how I feel about dying by lethal injection?"

"No, I was going to ask you if you'd thought about trying to make a plea bargain deal with the prosecutor, dumb ass."

"No, frankly I have not." Chilcott was silent for a moment, then asked, "Seriously, do you think I should?" It struck Chilcott that, as much as a pain in the ass Carlisle was, he probably had a lot of experience with criminal law.

"I'd say you're a dumb ass if you don't."

"My public defender mentioned it when we first met, but hasn't said anything about the possibility of a plea bargain since the arraignment."

Red Bone snorted. "If you're willing to trust a PD with your life, then you're crazier than I am."

"I'm supposed to see him later this week. I'll discuss it with him then," Chilcott said thoughtfully.

"Good. You better be thinking about what sentence you would be willing to accept for a plea deal," Carlisle advised.

"Maybe you should have studied law instead of BS at your alma mater."

"Yeah, but I only made it through the ninth grade. The school principal threw me out for fighting and I never returned to school," Carlisle paused a second, then added,

"Maybe I should have gone back."

"You're probably right," Chilcott said.

"Right about what? Don't you know by now that Red Bone is always right!"

"Yeah, sure you are. I just meant to say that I agreed with you. I'll tell the guards I want to see my lawyer right away. Just for my information, Carlisle, what's your real name?"

"If you must know, my real name is Carlisle Pickering. But sometimes people just call me Doc."

What a screwball. I'm afraid to ask why they call him Doc. "I think I'll just call you Carlisle," Chilcott said. "It's less confusing."

"That would probably be a good idea, dumb ass," Carlisle said. "I'll talk to you later."

* * *

The following morning, Chilcott met with his attorney, Willard Berry, to discuss the possibility of going to the prosecutor with a deal. Chilcott asked Berry whether the prosecutor would consider a deal such as, in return for a guilty plea to second degree murder and dropping the drug charges, Chilcott would agree to a sentence of 20-years. Berry agreed to propose the offer. "I'll let you know what he says later today," Berry promised.

Chilcott anxiously awaited Berry's return. When Berry

finally returned later in the day, Chilcott noticed that his attorney wasn't smiling. "How did it go, Mr. Berry?" Chilcott asked nervously.

"Not very well. I had hoped he might be willing to work with me. Instead, he just laughed and said, "No deal. If your client will accept a 40-year sentence, I'd seriously consider a plea."

Chilcott gulped, then asked quietly, "Mr. Berry, what do you think?"

"I think he's fishing to see how long of a sentence you'd be willing to accept," Berry replied.

"I've got another idea. Tell him I'd agree to a 25-year sentence for second degree murder, if he agrees to drop the drug charges. And, as an added bonus, I'd include information that would help them solve the Rachael Miller homicide case."

"Are you involved with that murder too?" Berry asked in a tone of shock and surprise.

"No, not directly. But I know something they'll probably never find out without my help."

"Well, I'm glad of that," Berry said sounding relieved.

"Make the offer and get back to me in the morning, will you please?" Chilcott requested.

"I'll do it," Berry said. "I will remind Prosecutor Murphy that the minimum sentence for second degree murder is 15 years to life, but with the possibility of parole. And, I'll also remind him that the evidence presented so far is mostly circumstantial. Murphy has no eye witnesses to rely on, so he ought to be willing to make a deal."

* * *

The next day, Berry returned with good news. "At first, the prosecutor told me he wanted to make an example out of you, since you are a cop. He was planning to throw the book at you. But when I suggested a compromise of 25 years, and told him of your willingness to help solve the Rachael Miller case, Prosecutor Murphy became very interested. I'm certain your offer to help solve the Miller case did the trick. He told me he was willing to accept the deal as long as your testimony about the case will be truthful and accurate. I assured him that it will be. So, he agreed to the deal." Berry studied his client, and then asked, "Are you willing to go through with that plea agreement?"

"Well, I'm happy he accepted the deal. I'm not happy about doing that much time in prison, but I guess that's the way it goes, huh counselor?"

"I understand, but it's better than facing life imprisonment without parole or a lethal injection. You should be very thankful for that. You'll probably only have to do a little more than 12-years, so long as you get time off for good behavior."

"Yeah, I know you're right. Serving time and getting paroled is better than dying or being imprisoned for life."

"Glad you agree. So, later today we'll meet with the

prosecutor. You'll sign off on the plea agreement, and then give your sworn testimony about the Rachael Miller case. After the judge accepts the deal, you'll be done. No more worries about the risk of what could happen at a trial. After the sentencing hearing, you'll be transferred to Columbus, where the Ohio State Penitentiary is located. It's a super-max prison that's been around for years. It houses over 500 prisoners. Most of the inmates are there for committing murder. So, you'll need to be careful and watch out for yourself," Berry advised.

"Thank you very much for your help, Mr. Berry," Chilcott said as he extended his hand and shook his attorney's out stretched hand.

Berry gathered his paperwork and case file off the conference room table and said, "I'm glad we could resolve these legal proceedings for you, Randy. Do yourself a favor and stay out of trouble in Columbus."

"Yes, that's what I intend to do. I'll keep my head down and maybe I'll see you in about 12 years, when I'm released from prison."

"You probably will, because I intend to continue practicing law for 15 more years or as long as my health is good."

Chapter 26

A week later, early Thursday morning on March 30, 1989, Grant County Sheriff, Roger Jackson went into the Detective Bureau and left a large envelope on Captain Clarence Moore's desk. When Moore entered his office at 7:30 a.m. he immediately noticed the plain legal-size manila envelope lying on top of his desk. He opened the envelope. Inside was a typed statement from Randy Chilcott and a signed and file-stamped plea agreement in the case of State of Ohio v. Randall T. Chilcott. The agreement stated that Chilcott agreed to plead guilty to second degree murder. The State agreed to request the Court impose no more than a 25-year sentence and to allow parole. Both parties requested the Court to dismiss the drug charges. The agreement was signed by the Grant County Prosecutor, Samuel Murphy, the Defendant, Randall T. Chilcott, and Attorney Willard Berry. The agreement bore the signature and seal of Grant County Circuit Court Judge Lawrence Wilson. The document was file-stamped and dated that day, March 30, 1989. The enclosed statement signed by Chilcott concerning the Rachael Miller homicide case was dated March 22, 1989.

Moore excitedly began to read Chilcott's statement about the Rachael Miller case. Chilcott's statement attested that on the evening of December 27, 1988, he was told by Monica Kerlin that she had been outside Jacob Moore's barn, looking through a window on the evening of December 19, 1988. The statement described what Kerlin had told Chilcott she'd seen.

The statement was fairly lengthy and Moore hurriedly read through the document. He learned that Monica was at the barn to deliver marijuana to James Miller. She had parked Chilcott's Oldsmobile in the dirt access road adjacent to the barn. Chilcott stated that Monica had sold marijuana to James on previous occasions, but not at his residence. She agreed to deliver the contraband to the Miller farm on condition that James would pay an additional amount to the normal price for two "dime bags". She informed Chilcott that she had made it clear to James that delivery to his home was only a one-time occurrence and that she was doing him a favor, because she expected him to introduce her to other Amish customers. Chilcott's statement also claimed that in early December, 1988, Monica burglarized several rural properties in and around Grant County. He stated that she intended to continue her burglary spree and pot-selling business, and that he ended her life, in part, to put an end to her criminal activity.

Moore snorted in disbelief at his former side-kick's attempt to justify the murder of his girlfriend. *But what the hell, she was dead and Randy was going to do a long bit in the slammer.* He was rushing through the statement anxious to get to the part describing what Monica had seen through the window pane. For months Moore had

www.ingramcontent.com/pod-product-compliance
Lightning Source LLC
LaVergne TN
LVHW091034080826
845145LV00002B/493

9781771434690

investigation of the death of Rachael Miller. He recalled saying how impressed he was with Chilcott's knowledge of the country roads and asking him if he'd been to the Millers' house before. Moore also remembered his first reaction to the "crime scene". He had wondered whether Rachael might have been in the barn pleasuring herself and had accidentally fallen when she got up. *Well, I guess I was partially right.*

Later that morning, Moore arrived at the Miller farm unexpectedly. He wanted to talk to Jacob and Sarah Miller and to their son, James. When he pulled into their driveway the elder Miller saw Moore approaching and waited beside the gravel driveway.

Moore exited his vehicle and shook the Amish man's extended hand. Moore explained that he had news about Rachael's case that he wanted to share with the family. Moore could tell that Jacob was both anxious and fearful to learn what the news would reveal. Nevertheless, Jacob invited him in and Sarah poured him a cup of hot tea. Miller told one of the younger kids, who was in the kitchen, to go get James. "Tell him his mother and I want to talk to him inside the house right away," the elder Miller said.

When James arrived inside the house, he was surprised to find Detective Moore and his father and mother waiting for him at the kitchen table. Moore began, "I have a written statement attesting to the fact that James had nothing to do with pushing Rachael back against the spike which led to her tragic death on the night of December 19, 1988. It appears she accidentally fell backwards onto the spike and died as a result of the injury to her brain stem.

A look of absolute relief was visible on all three of the Millers' faces sitting at the table with Moore. Moore went on to say, "The investigation into her death has been concluded and any implication of guilt is removed from your family. I'm sorry she died and relieved that I've been able to unravel the true facts and put this very complex case to an end. I'm just sorry it took me so long to do it."

As Moore looked across the table, he saw tears well up in James' eyes and he was shaking his head in relief. *I'm sure James is wondering why I didn't bring up his involvement the night Rachael died. I didn't mention it to his parents because part of the truth had already been revealed. And, according to the Amish beliefs, James would be forgiven for his sinful behavior, provided he was repentant. But James was always going to be looked upon and remembered by his family as a liar and as an incestuous fornicator. That was enough punishment for anyone,* Moore thought. *Regardless, I'm glad and thankful that James wasn't a killer as well.*

Detective Moore thanked Mr. and Mrs. Miller for their cooperation, got up from the table, and said his goodbyes. Once outside, he climbed into his unmarked police cruiser and headed back to his office. He knew there were more cases in his in-basket to investigate and the residents of Grant County, the Sheriff, and the Prosecutor were all waiting for him to solve them. *I'm glad I relocated to Grant County,* he thought. *It turns out our change of residence was a good move to make*, he told himself as he drove away.

speculated about whether one of the Miller family members killed Rachael, and, if so, which one. He thought the guilty party was most likely James, but wondered whether another family member was also involved.

Chilcott described the scene in the barn so vividly it seemed like he'd been there himself, Moore thought. *Is it possible Randy was actually there with Monica? If so, why didn't he just say he had seen it too? I suppose he wanted to avoid implicating himself in selling drugs, so Murphy would agree to drop those charges.*

Chilcott's statement described the scene outside the barn as Kerlin looked through the small glass window pane. Chilcott claimed that she described to him in detail what she saw that night at the Miller farm around 8:15 p.m. James was smoking a joint and handed it to a young Amish girl, who stood next to him in the barn. There was a faint light from a kerosene lantern that illuminated the space. Kerlin said she wondered whether the girl was James' sister or someone else. Kerlin was just about ready to stop looking through the window and leave, when she saw James pull down his pants and his underwear. So, Kerlin was curious to see what was going to happen next.

She watched as the girl started to unbutton her coat and unclasp her dress, revealing her white panties and brassiere. The couple started kissing and sexually caressing each other. Soon, she saw James' hand slip under her breast and lift the bra up exposing one small breast. As the sexual acts continued, Chilcott claimed that Kerlin told him it was turning her on. After a minute or so, James' hand moved toward the girl's vagina. Then, the girl dropped her panties. The girl laid a blanket on the floor in front of several bundles of hay and quickly lay down on her back and opened her legs.

Chilcott claimed Kerlin saw James lie down with the girl to have sexual intercourse with her. But then, Kerlin moved closer to the dirt-covered window for a better view and she slipped on some ice on the ground next to the barn. The noise outside apparently startled the couple, because James quickly got up and pulled his underwear and pants back on. He said something in German to the girl, turned, and ran toward the barn door. James opened the door and rushed out of the barn leaving the girl to fend for herself.

The young Amish girl looked startled as she started to buckle up her dress before rising. She was still struggling to arrange her clothing as she stood up, but then she lost her balance and fell backwards toward one of the large barn posts. Chilcott stated that Kerlin didn't know what happened to the girl until afterwards, when he told her about the homicide investigation on the evening of December 20, 1988.

Once James left the barn, Kerlin informed Chilcott that she'd also swiftly walked back to the 83 Oldsmobile parked on the dirt road. She saw the Amish girl accidentally fall, but had no idea she'd died. Moore said to himself, *it's all beginning to make sense. Rachael died because she lost her balance and fell on the spike. There was no homicide and James wasn't responsible for her death. It was an accident on Rachael's part.*

Moore remembered his comment to Chilcott, when they were driving to the Miller farm at the beginning of the